"I'll sleep on the floor."

Char made the suggestion as she and Adam surveyed the tiny bedroom. The only bed was a small cot.

"I'm not going to take the bed while you sleep on the floor," Adam stated flatly. "But we could open your sleeping bag and spread it on the floor as a makeshift mattress."

Char looked right at him. "That means sleeping together."

Adam looked right back. "Uh-huh. It does."

The lighthearted mood was suddenly gone. Char could feel the heat in his eyes. They were finished playing games. "Adam, I don't want to ruin our friendship...."

"What friendship?" he asked, slipping his arms around her. "You and I have barely tolerated each other for years. Seems to me we must have just been waiting for lightning to strike."

As Adam's mouth found hers, Char knew he was right. Lightning *was* about to strike....

Carla Neggers just had to do it! She had to return to Millbrook, Vermont, the historic mill town setting of *Finders Keepers*, and continue the story of the Stiles family. Carla's fans will be delighted to know that the fun doesn't stop with *Within Reason*. The third book in the series will be available in April 1991. That's three times the laughter, three times the romance. All from one of Temptation's most popular authors.

Books by Carla Neggers

HARLEQUIN TEMPTATION

108—CAPTIVATED
162—TRADE SECRETS
190—FAMILY MATTERS
208—ALL IN A NAME
236—A WINNING BATTLE
275—FINDERS KEEPERS

Within Reason

CARLA NEGGERS

Harlequin Books

TORONTO • NEW YORK • LONDON
AMSTERDAM • PARIS • SYDNEY • HAMBURG
STOCKHOLM • ATHENS • TOKYO • MILAN

To Don and Paula,
and to Millie and Larry

Published December 1990

ISBN 0-373-25428-8

WITHIN REASON

———————— **1** ————————

"ONLY YOU, CHAR."

Adam Stiles could hear the lack of affection—not to mention patience—in his voice as he sat behind the wheel of his rented car. It was early autumn in Nashville, the weather hot and steamy. He had switched off the air-conditioning and rolled down the window to get a better look at the Belle Meade Mansion. He'd parked in the visitors' lot and left the engine running, a sign, he supposed, of just how much he didn't want to do what he was doing.

Squinting, he looked across the oak-shaded lawn. The antebellum mansion had clean Greek Revival lines and an air of old Southern aristocracy that should have had a calming effect on his nerves. It didn't. Nothing Charity Winnifred Bradford did had ever had a calming effect on his nerves. And she was directly responsible for his sweating to death in a rented car, staring at a popular Tennessee tourist attraction and wondering what the hell Char was up to this time.

With a grunt of irritation, he snatched the photograph she had sent home off the passenger seat. He didn't need another look, but he took one, anyway. The house across the lawn and the house in the photo were the same.

He flipped it over and read the address neatly printed on the back: 110 Leake Avenue, seven miles southwest of downtown Nashville. In her more normal scrawl, Char had added, *Come see me!*

She hadn't meant him. That much Adam knew. Whatever he and Char were, they couldn't be called friends. For as long as he could remember they had argued about the merits of life in the hills of southern Vermont. He saw many positives; Char saw none, or to be totally accurate one: the area was, she had to allow, pretty. But she would add, perverse woman that she was, how much scenic beauty can a person stand? She was training and breeding horses in Tennessee these days, she'd told everyone in her hometown of Millbrook. Not just regular old horses, either. Thoroughbreds. *Winners.* One had Triple Crown written all over him.

Charity Winnifred Bradford had always been a levelheaded woman not prone to exaggeration. Irascible, direct and often irritating, she had, nevertheless, a good head on her shoulders. She just didn't do crazy things. But who knew what horse fever did to people?

Not that it was any of Adam's business, as Char would be the first to tell him. If she wanted to live in a beautiful Southern mansion and raise horses, that was her affair.

Still, here he was.

Seldom at a loss for action, Adam didn't know what to do next. Char had been impossible as long as anyone in Millbrook could remember. Apparently a year in the mid-South hadn't changed her—not that anything would. She was argumentative, stubborn, independent, resourceful and blunt. And smart. He had to give her that.

She was also his sister Beth's best friend from way back, and Adam had promised he'd look in on her while he was in Nashville on business. He hadn't understood why Beth was worried. For one thing, Char had to be doing all right if she lived in that big mansion in the photograph she had sent Beth. For another, if there was anyone in this world who could damn well take care of herself, it was Charity Bradford.

Beth being Beth, she had persisted, and Adam had finally given in. His business in Nashville on behalf of Mill Brook Post & Beam, the sawmill and manufacturers of high-quality housing kits owned by the Stiles family, wasn't all-consuming. And, like most people in Millbrook, he owed Charity Bradford, no matter how much she bugged him or how much she would scoff at the idea. For the past five years she had been one of Millbrook's very few lawyers and its very best. She was known in her practice for being closemouthed, tenacious and absolutely convincing. People—Adam included—had assumed she had come home to stay.

People had been wrong. So had he.

He set down the photograph of the picturesque Greek Revival house, put the car in park and switched off the ignition. He opened the door on the driver's side with the hook that was now his left hand—when he chose to wear it. Often he didn't, having found he could get along just fine without it. As his attorney, Char had helped him sort through the legal and insurance nightmares in the aftermath of his wife's death and his own crippling accident, coming so quickly on the heels of each other. Char had been briskly professional and efficient, he recalled, if not particularly sensitive. "Losing a hand's pretty bad," she'd told him, "but you'd get more for a foot."

He'd remarked he'd keep that in mind should any of his three remaining appendages get near a Mill Brook

Post & Beam saw. Instead of having the grace to flush, Char had looked at him with those doe-brown eyes of hers and burst out laughing at her own insensitivity.

"Am I jerk or what?" she'd asked rhetorically, her self-deprecation underlined with a healthy self-confidence.

Adam had found himself laughing, too. Thinking back, he couldn't recall why: Char wasn't a funny woman. But he had laughed, and it had felt good. For the first time in many months he had felt wholly human again.

He headed up the walk, wishing he had left his hook back at the hotel and worn a short-sleeved shirt. The combination of the hook apparatus, his long-sleeved work shirt and the oppressive humidity had him feeling damn uncomfortable. The prospect of barging in on sweet Charity Bradford unannounced didn't help. If she were playing games with her family and friends about where she lived, she wouldn't want any spies poking around, then heading back home and countering her claims. Adam felt for all her faults, he did know Char. Even at her sweetest the woman could make a rattlesnake sweat.

A breeze stirred the humid air as he followed the signs to the gift shop adjoining the mansion. Once there, he scanned a brochure that explained Belle Meade was formerly a fifty-three-hundred-acre plantation that, in the nineteenth century, had been a world-famous Thoroughbred nursery and stud. Twenty-four acres of the original plantation remained. In addition to the house there were a dairy, smokehouse, garden house and carriage house and stalls.

It was owned by the Association for the Preservation of Tennessee Antiquities, not by a prickly ex-Yankee Adam had known all her thirty-three years.

He wandered around the gift shop while debating his next move. His kids would have loved the place, but they were having a grand time for themselves with their Uncle Julian and new Aunt Holly. Adam had never gone in for mixing business and family vacations. Even this short side trip violated his normal operating procedure, but he consoled himself with a reminder that although stopping in to see Char might not be business, it certainly wasn't pleasure. It was a favor to his sister. Period.

Finally he decided subtlety wasn't going to work and asked the woman behind the counter if she knew Charity Bradford. The woman, middle-aged and very proper, apologized that she didn't know anyone by that name. Adam resisted telling her no apology was necessary. In fact, she should be delighted Char's path and her own had never crossed. For sure, she'd have recalled.

Instead he thanked her politely, bought a packet of fake Confederate money for his daughter Abby and his son David and headed back into the warm Tennessee afternoon.

Whatever pot Char had boiling, Adam decided he wasn't going to jump into it. She was Beth's friend. So let Beth find her.

He walked back to his car, wishing he felt more relieved.

JUST BEFORE FIVE that morning Char had begun to suspect it was going to be one of *those* days. It was the tent this time. While she was dreaming of better days and

Emily was sacked out with that peaceful I-trust-you-Mom expression that could slice a mother's heart in two, their tent had collapsed on them. Emily, a precocious seven, had taken the calamity in stride. Char, a cynical thirty-three, had not. She had known someone like Adam Stiles would blunder into her life before the day was out.

Peering out from behind a marble column of the pre-Civil War house she'd stupidly—arrogantly—claimed as her own, she watched Adam head to the visitors' parking lot. Even from the back he couldn't be anything else but a strong man from a small town in southern Vermont, a taciturn, stolid, unimaginative Yankee whose heart and soul—whose life—was Mill Brook Post & Beam. He would never even consider risking it all on a dream. A man like Adam didn't dream. Dreams weren't a part of his practical nature. Why should they be? He didn't need dreams. His life was exactly what he wanted it to be.

Then her gaze dropped to the hook that had become his left hand, and she remembered the car accident that had killed his wife, Mel. Char exhaled, suddenly feeling tired. She recalled those dark, sad, harsh days after Mel's death, with Adam's grief, his guilt, so palpable to everyone in Millbrook.

Like Char, Mel had wanted out of Millbrook, but in a different way, for different reasons. Mel had always been an outsider in town and had refused to think of Millbrook as home. Not so with Char. Claustrophobic, beautiful, sometimes stimulating, Millbrook *was* home to her. Mel's dream of leaving had been a woman's dream; she'd come to Millbrook as an adult when she married Adam Stiles. Char's dream of leaving was wrapped up in her childhood, in the hopes and longings she'd had as a girl while listening to the pitter-patter of rain on her dormer roof. She had gotten out. Not so Mel. She had died in Millbrook, and for a long time the man she had married had blamed himself for her unhappiness. Char wasn't going to let that happen to the people who cared about her: she was responsible for her own happiness.

And her own misery.

Maybe Adam's life wasn't perfect, but he was the kind of person who accepted whatever life threw at him with a stiff upper lip. No complaining from Adam Stiles. No grasping for impossible dreams. No, not Adam. He would never understand why Char had risked so much, not just to get out of Vermont, but to chase a childhood dream.

All of which was beside the point. Char didn't give a damn if Adam dreamed or didn't dream. Nor did she care if he thought she was nuts. The point was, she knew Adam, and the Adam Stiles she knew wasn't going to give up on her and go back to Vermont.

That was a dream. He might *like* to give up: he and Char had never had much use for each other. But in addition to being taciturn, stolid and practical, Adam Stiles was also relentless. By now he had a fair idea his sister's best friend didn't live at 110 Leake Avenue just southwest of downtown Nashville, Tennessee. Adam being Adam, he'd want to know exactly where Char *did* live.

One thing about camping out in a tent, she wouldn't be easy to find.

Char waited until Adam had climbed into his car and cleared off Belle Meade property before she raced back to the gift shop where she worked part-time, thanked her friend there for covering for her, reassured her everything was fine and headed back out toward her own car, such as it was.

She was free. Adam was gone, and he wasn't going to find her. The crisis was over. Char found herself feeling not so much giddy at having avoided him, but oddly depressed. No, she thought, depressed was too strong. Just emotional, she decided. Ridiculously nostalgic. More than anyone else she could think of, Adam Stiles represented the life she'd given up—the life she'd deliberately rejected. Small-town New England, ice-cold winters, the claustrophobic yet beautiful mountains of Vermont, the places and smells and sounds that had been a part of her for so long. *Too* long. There was no going back. She'd said that a year ago, with such bravado and hope. Now she knew it to be so.

Home...

She blinked back tears, annoyed with herself. Home wasn't Millbrook, Vermont. It wasn't even central Tennessee. She'd learned the hard way that home was, simply, wherever she and Emily were.

"Oh, no."

Her words came out in a whisper, loud enough just for her to hear. Her knees stiffened and her mouth went dry, all anger and nostalgia dispersed.

Adam Stiles was leaning against the rusting door of her 1980 hatchback.

He hadn't left Belle Meade after all. The sneak had doubled back and found her car. Now he was observing her with a proprietary air that set her teeth on edge.

Never one to reveal her feelings to an adversary, Char recovered her poise and, with a frankness that she hoped matched his, took a good, long look at this man who'd always been, if only peripherally, a part of her life. She hadn't seen him in a year, but that made little difference: Adam Stiles just wasn't one to change. He wore the same boots he'd worn for the past ten years, the same kind of close-fitting jeans, the same kind of soft chambray work shirt. Although he'd add a jacket and a tie as needed, even sometimes put on wool trousers and a dress shirt, Char couldn't recall ever having seen him in a suit.

She noticed the sunlight dancing on the silver highlights in his hair and casting shadows over his blue-green eyes, bringing out the sharp angles of his face. He was more a hard, solid man than a good-looking one. If Char were going to be objective—and she seldom was where Adam Stiles was concerned—she'd have to admit he was unconscionably sexy in an unaffected yet totally unyielding way. It wasn't anything deliberate on his part; it was just Adam. When she was twelve and he nineteen, Char had had a mindless, ultrasecret crush on him, one of those embarrassing episodes of childhood she'd smartly kept to herself. Not even Beth had known. Adam certainly hadn't. As far as he was concerned, Char had always had the same opinion of him she did now, which was just short of active dislike. He was too Millbrook, too silent, too damn *boring*. Their attorney-client relationship had been professional, never buddy-buddy, Adam never anything more than her best friend's older brother.

Now he was a problem. Potentially a big problem.

Coming closer, she saw that the hook seemed more natural than it had a year ago, more a part of him. Once it had been a terrible reminder of his wife's tragic death and his own tortured state in the months afterward when he'd had his first and thus far only mishap with one of the mill's huge saws. *Maybe he's finally put the past behind him*, Char speculated, mildly surprised at her interest. But she rationalized that he *was* Beth's brother and someone Char herself had known forever. Her interest was just natural.

Char suddenly wondered if Adam had started seeing women again since she'd left Millbrook. He'd always struck her as a one-woman man, and Mel, for better or worse, had been his one woman. Knowing Adam as she did, Char didn't expect him to rush out and repeat the experience of marriage. But she couldn't believe he'd go on forever without some kind of female companionship, if for no other reason than there were too many single women in New England angling for his attention for him not to notice eventually. He was human, after all. Or was someone going to have to tell him that? It had been more than three years since Mel's death, and not one rumor of Adam and another woman had ever reached Char.

He squinted at her in the hazy sunshine. "Hello, Char."

She didn't turn and run, but acknowledged without surprise that the urge was there. Adam could be one hell of an intimidating man. Instead she remained where she was and squinted right back at him, intensely aware not just of him, but of herself—her lies, her life, her appearance. For one of the few times in her life she felt self-conscious. She knew what Adam saw: a woman two months shy of thirty-four, with round brown eyes, too pert a nose for her taste, a wide mouth and bobbed brown hair. Not dramatically beautiful, but not homely, either. If he were looking—and since they'd known each other forever she doubted he'd bother— he'd see her high, well-shaped breasts and notice that her long legs, by far her best feature, were thinner than they had been a year ago. She had on the same outfit she'd had on when she'd stopped by the mill to say goodbye to Beth on her way out of town: a madras skirt, white shirt and sandals. Would Adam remember?

She managed a broad smile that she hoped radiated her strong personality and natural self-confidence. "Welcome to Belle Meade."

"Going to invite me in?" he asked mildly.

Nothing in his expression or tone indicated anything but total sincerity. Which, of course, had the effect of making his request seem that much more sarcastic. Typical Adam Stiles. Char, however, remained unruffled. Unlike most everyone else in southern Vermont, she never had found Adam particularly scary, perhaps because she so obviously bugged him. "He can barely remember the names of my other friends," Beth used to tell her, "but you, Char—you he remembers." It hadn't been Adam's idea of a compliment.

"Sorry," she said, straight-faced. "I can't invite you in. I have guests."

He dropped his eyes slightly, taking in all of her, the sunlight catching the blue-gree of his irises. His expression didn't change. He was, Char knew, an imposing man. She stood her ground.

His eyes fastened back on hers, and he said calmly, "Why Belle Meade?"

Feigning innocence wasn't her long suit, but she gave it a shot. "What do you mean?"

"You might have gotten away with something smaller, not as well-known." He nodded back toward the impressive mansion. "This is a bit much, Char, even for you."

Her innocent act hadn't prompted even a second's hesitation on his part. Obviously it wasn't going to work, not with him. Char shrugged. "I always go for broke."

His eyes flashed, warning her he'd heard the unintended bitterness in her voice. She'd have to be more careful, especially with him, although caution wasn't her style. College in Boston, law school in New York, her first job in Manhattan, her doomed marriage to a rising corporate lawyer, Tennessee—all were products of her compulsion to take risks, to dream. Only going back to Millbrook for those interminable five years after her divorce had been practical and safe. She'd had stability in Vermont. A burgeoning practice, a house, a bank account, a happy child...

"How's Emily?" Adam asked quietly, breaking into her troubled thoughts.

"Great. I've got to pick her up—"

"Didn't you tell Beth you'd hired a Mary Poppins?"

She'd told Beth a lot of things. "My Peruvian nanny? She's wonderful, but she's on vacation at the moment. Em's visiting a friend."

Adam slid away from her car and stood in front of Char, so close she could take in every detail of him, every nuance of his seventy-four inches. He had always been a powerfully built man, but she didn't remember him being so damn tall—a full head taller than she. If asked that morning, she would have said they were about the same height.

"You're a liar, Char," he told her matter-of-factly. "Always have been."

She managed a grin. "Keeps me alert."

"How come you avoided me back at the gift shop?"

"What woman in her right mind wouldn't?"

He nodded at that, making no argument. "I recognized your car as I passed by. Otherwise I'd have missed you."

"Lucky me," she said, not too sarcastically. She wasn't afraid of Adam, but she didn't want to annoy him. He might decide to get his revenge by meddling in her life and finding out more things he had no business finding out. *I want him to go back home and leave me alone. Really, I do.*

He let her comment slide. "Funny, a rich lady like you driving the same old bomb you've always driven. You remind me of Beth."

"That's not fair. The fact is, Beth's car's a good fifteen years older than mine."

Adam wasn't impressed. "Living in an antebellum mansion, you should at least have a decent car."

"Are you teasing me?" she asked in surprise. Julian, Adam's younger brother and the middle Stiles, was the teaser in the family. Adam just didn't know how, or so Char had always thought.

"Just commenting on the 'facts,' as you call them."

What was *that* supposed to mean? "Well, I'm not into conspicuous consumption."

"Except when it comes to houses?"

She dug her keys out of her handbag. "Really, I have to go. Em'll start worrying."

"Dinner?" Adam asked suddenly, his eyes widening slightly, holding her in place as surely as if he'd grabbed her.

A firm no was on Char's lips. She hadn't had dinner with Adam in years. When she had, Beth or Julian or his kids or his parents—somebody—had always been around. What would she say to him? What would he say to her? They would end up talking houses and cars and Vermont. He would ask her questions. His invitation had to be part of a plot to wheedle more information from her about her life in Tennessee. He didn't *want* to have dinner. If nothing else, he was just fulfilling his sense of duty to his sister. In fact, Char could probably thank Beth for this entire visit.

Definitely, Char thought, she should say no and get rid of Adam Stiles ASAP.

But, honorable and duty-bound individual that Adam Stiles was, since he had done the inviting, he would consider picking up the tab his responsibility. Free food, Char cautioned herself, was free food. It had been weeks since she and Emily had been out on the town. Longer, even. Adam's company was the price they would have to pay for the pleasure. Was it too high a price?

"I can bring Em?"

"Sure. You choose the place. What time?"

"Six, if that's not too early. Em poops out by eight."

"Fine. Where should I pick you up?"

"I can meet you—"

He shook his head in that stubborn Yankee way of his.

Char sighed. "Right out at the front gate, then."

"Here?"

"Where else?"

He started toward her. "Char..."

She smiled and quickly unlocked the driver's door to her car. "We'll be waiting."

CHAR COULDN'T GET AWAY from Belle Meade and Adam Stiles fast enough, but she hit the brakes at an upscale shopping center in the wealthy suburban town of Belle Meade, located on land that had once been part of the former plantation, and found a pay phone. She called Beth Stiles in Vermont, collect. They had been best friends since nursery school; Beth had always been the one person Char could count on and trust. They used to climb trees as kids and plot how they were going to get out of Millbrook and do something with their lives.

Char gave Beth just enough time to accept the charges before she started in. "Why'd you sic your big brother on me?"

Beth didn't even hesitate. "Because you haven't invited me to your place in Tennessee and I got to wondering just what it is you aren't telling me."

"I've been busy, that's all."

"Then how come you're so upset about seeing Adam, and how come you're calling me collect? Come on, Char. Something's up."

"*Adam's* up—you know he drives me nuts. I wasn't thinking straight when I called collect. I'm sorry. I'll send a check in the morning to cover the bill."

"Don't be ridiculous. And you're just blowing smoke. Level with me, okay? What's going on?"

Char took a deep breath, composing herself before she said something she would regret later. She and Beth had seldom kept secrets from each other, but there was a time for everything. "You don't have to worry about me," she said coolly, sounding more like her old lawyer self than she had in months. "So call off your brother, all right?"

"You're starting to sound paranoid. What's Adam done to you?"

"Nothing—yet. He just has that know-it-all mountain man way about him. You know how he is. Beth, please call him off."

"Char." Beth exhaled. "Everything's okay with our little enterprise, isn't it?"

Char bristled, feeling trapped and guilty, but she managed to say smoothly, "Yes, of course. You didn't tell Adam about it, did you?"

"Of course not. I'm not *that* crazy."

"Thank heavens," Char said, unable to hide her relief. "Look, Beth, everything's fine. I just don't want Adam poking around in my life right now. You know how he is. He'll *never* understand why I left Millbrook. And I don't have time to waste trying to explain. So quit worrying and—"

"It's not the worse thing in the world to have someone worry about you, and I can't help it. We're your friends, Char. Adam, too, in his own way. You can't hide from us..."

"I'm not hiding! Listen, I've got to run. We'll talk again soon."

And she hung up before Beth could say another word. Char hadn't liked the note of suspicion—and concern—that had crept into her friend's voice. If they had continued their conversation, Char undoubtedly would have said something to convince Beth she had done the right thing in siccing Adam on her, which was all Char needed. Then Beth would call her brother and urge him to keep bugging Char until he had all the facts. Then, Char thought dismally, where would I be?

"Not much worse off than I already am," she muttered to herself.

There was still, she didn't need to remind herself, dinner ahead with Adam Stiles. She must have been nuts to have walked into that trap! It wasn't as if she didn't know what she was getting into. All those years in Millbrook, Vermont, had left her with a clear notion of who and what Adam Stiles was.

She'd just jumped out of the frying pan and into the fire was what she'd done.

At least the evening wasn't going to cost her anything.

Not financially, anyway. Her nerves and her pride could suffer, but what did they matter anymore? The gnawing in her stomach, from another in a series of skipped lunches, told her that what counted now was food. And she couldn't wait to tell Emily they were having dinner out. Little gadabout that she was, she'd be thrilled.

Climbing back into her car, Char turned her mind to considering the options of just where she would have Adam take them for dinner. There were a zillion good restaurants in the Nashville area, most of which she had only read about. Her mouth watered. She'd been eating healthy foods lately; *lots* of legumes. What she wanted now, she decided, was a nice, thick, juicy, cholesterol- and fat-ladened steak.

A couple of hours of Adam Stiles surely wasn't too high a price to pay for such a treat.

"DID CHAR TELL YOU Belle Meade's a museum?" Adam sat on the edge of the king-size bed in his hotel suite as he spoke to his sister. He had taken a long, therapeutic swim, trying to put Char temporarily out of his mind, before calling Beth. "I'll send you a brochure."

"Adam, what the hell's going on?"

"You tell me."

"I don't know anything to tell you! Look, I'm worried. Char might hate me for it, but I have to know what's going on with her. I know you are like fire and water, but—" Beth broke off, frustrated. "Adam, normal people don't tell their friends they live in museum houses."

"Since when has Char ever been a normal person?"

But he sighed, relenting, if only because his business in Tennessee wasn't nearly as interesting as Charity Bradford's apparent secrets. Not to mention his sister's. That Beth had left out a few pertinent details regarding her wayward friend was obvious to Adam, who wasn't the only one to find his sister an easy read. Her honest nature was appealing and often helpful in business, but also, on occasion, got her into trouble. She was a lousy liar. Adam, however, had decided back in Millbrook when he'd accepted Beth's mission that he wasn't going to browbeat her for the truth. If Beth wanted to tell him what the hell was going on, she'd get around to it. If not, he'd pry it out of her one fact at a time . . . or he'd get it from Char.

"This isn't going to be easy," he went on. "You know that, don't you?"

"Yeah, I guess I do. Char plays everything close to the chest—one reason she's such a good lawyer. Maybe this Belle Meade thing was a joke, but you know Char. She's never been much of a prankster."

A vision of Charity Bradford, J.D., dressed in one of her power suits and withering the other side in a courtroom battle seeped its way into Adam's mind. No, Char wasn't known for her sense of humor. Sending Beth a picture of a museum house and saying she lived there wasn't Millbrook's favorite hard-case lawyer's idea of a joke.

So why had she done it?

"Okay, Beth," he said, "I'll see what I can find out."

"Thanks, Adam."

"I'm taking her to dinner tonight—"

"What?"

Adam frowned at the shock in his sister's voice. "I said I'm taking her to dinner tonight. How cheap do you think I am?"

But Beth was silent.

"Beth?"

"It is bad, Adam. She's in trouble. I know she is. For Char to agree to let *anyone* take her to dinner is a near miracle. You know how she is about paying her own way in the world. But to let you of all people take her... it's got to be bad."

"Thanks a lot. But I think I know what you mean. Our sweet Charity has always preferred to give than to receive."

He could hear his own sarcasm and backed off: whatever her faults, Char *was* Beth's friend. But past irritations involving Charity Bradford weren't the only source of his sarcasm, and Adam knew he might as well admit it. The sarcasm rose, too, out of self-defense. Something about Char had gotten under his skin today. It had been as if he were seeing her for the first time. He had noticed the warm beauty of her eyes, the confidence and sauciness of her grin, the delicate curve of her breasts. The intelligence was still there, the toughness and the hotheadedness, but they weren't a surprise. Neither, if he thought about it, was the rest, only his reaction. For years he had seen Char simply as his younger sister's closest friend and Millbrook's most sought-after and intimidating lawyer, not as a complex and very attractive woman. Funny how he had never really thought of Char that way. Complex, attractive... desirable.

His swim had helped, but not enough.

"Look," he told his sister, "I'll do what I can to find out what's going on but Beth, Char's a grown woman. She has a right to her own life."

"I'm her friend," Beth snapped. "I have rights, too."

And what was he? Adam shook off the question. "Then I'll keep you posted."

"Good luck with dinner."

He nodded grimly. "Thanks. Knowing Char, I'm sure I'll need it."

2

CHAR AND EMILY arrived at Belle Meade ten minutes ahead of schedule. An afternoon thunderstorm had brought an all too temporary relief from the sultry air, and within minutes after the rain ended, Char felt her cotton shirt clinging to her back. Emily Bradford Williams, a slight, dark-eyed seven-year-old with straight tawny hair and crooked bangs—trimmed by her mother's own awkward fingers—was in a pout. She had wanted to wear her Vermont T-shirt with the Holstein on the front, but Char had put her foot down. She had also vetoed Emily's second choice, her Opryland T-shirt. Her father had bought it for her on his only trip to Tennessee, to see where his daughter was living. That had been months before the tent, which Char had explained to Emily was an adventure Daddy just would never understand.

When Emily finally dragged out one of the frilly, impossible dresses her paternal grandmother insisted on buying her, Char had had to give in. Emily, however, continued to feel put-upon.

"You don't have to stand around looking pretty," Char told her, guessing what the real issue at stake was. "Dresses wash."

Bingo.

Never one to hold a grudge for long, Emily took her mother at her word and started running around and all but turning somersaults. So much for prim and proper.

Two minutes before six Adam still hadn't arrived. Char half hoped, half dreaded that Beth had heeded her advice and called off her older brother and dinner was canceled. There would be no grilling, no dodging, no lying—but also no dinner. And, she had to admit, no touching base with somebody from Millbrook, Vermont, even if it was Adam Stiles.

Something annoyingly like relief washed over her when Adam pulled up to the curb in his rented car and climbed out, looking impatient and irritable and so damn sexy Char almost lost her breath. His occasional episodes of bad temper had never fazed her. His sexiness she'd never noticed. Now it was almost palpable—something she could touch with her hand. Maybe she was just reacting to the heat.

Before Char could say a word, Emily jumped forward, calling, "Uncle Adam, Uncle Adam!"

Ignoring Char, Adam crouched down in front of the little girl and greeted her with a warm hug, then pulled a couple of pictures from his wallet of Abby and David "from home" and presented her with a tiny box of maple sugar candy, also "from home." Pleasure radiated in Em's still-cherubic face. She thanked Uncle Adam profusely. She tore open the box and tried a piece of the candy. Then she looked up at her mother and said, "Mummy, he's not *that* mean."

Char pretended not to hear her daughter's remark and urged her into the back seat of the rented car, while Adam, coming up from his crouch, responded with a soft laugh. Char found his laughter oddly disturbing. She wasn't embarrassed by Emily's innocent betrayal: Adam had known Char's opinion of him years before her daughter had ever been born. No, she found his laugh disturbing because of what it did to the backs of her knees. It made them tingle. For the first time in her life she had to admit that the sawmill king of Mill-brook, Vermont, that stoic Yankee she'd known all her life, had an incorrigibly sexy laugh. Even when Char had had her mercifully brief crush on him at twelve, she hadn't been aware of his laughter doing anything to the backs of her knees.

Not a great start to an already potentially explosive evening. Perhaps, she thought, the tingling in the backs of her knees was just the result of her long day and the heat. That was the trick: blame the heat.

She shut the back door and let Emily tackle her seat belt alone, as was her customary wish. "I'm not a baby," she'd pronounced three years ago when Char had last tried to give her a hand. Fortunately Emily was more Bradford than Williams. Nick, born wearing cuff links and garters, was a decent enough man, but he hadn't understood Char, hadn't taken to becoming a father at twenty-six and had generally proved to be an unsym-pathetic presence in the lives of both his wife and daughter. Char was convinced Emily saw more of him since her parents' divorce than she would have had they remained married. Nick paid his child support on time—Char didn't have to remind him she was a law-yer—and he had Emily one weekend a month and two weeks in the summer, apparently just enough to sat-isfy all concerned. Emily understood her father and bore neither him nor her mother any ill will over a failed marriage she couldn't even remember. "Dad's just Dad," she would say. It was a charitable attitude Char encouraged, her own active animosity toward her ex-husband having faded as their years apart marched on.

"Aren't you going to get in?" Adam asked, breaking into her thoughts.

She scowled at him, but immediately regretted her own obvious bad mood. So far the man hadn't really done or said anything wrong. What was it about him that made her feel so damn defensive? *You can relax*, she told herself. *He doesn't know anything.*

Not yet.

He doesn't have to find out. You just need to be extra-careful.

"Char? You coming?"

She nodded. "I've had a long day. My mind was wandering."

He let it go at that, and Char climbed into the passenger seat. When was the last time she had been out with a man? It seemed like forever. She had been too busy, too preoccupied in the past year. Her social life had plummeted to the bottom of her list of concerns. In fact, it wasn't even *on* her list of concerns. And, in any case, having dinner with Adam Stiles wasn't like going out with a man. He was *Adam*. Beth's big brother. President of a family-owned sawmill business. A taciturn, isolated man with two children he adored. A Vermonter to his very core. The last thing he was was a date.

But she noticed the light, subtle scent of his cologne when he climbed into the car, and the well-developed muscles in his arms and shoulders. He'd put on a sport coat, but no tie. Ties weren't easy to negotiate with one hand. Still, he was dressed as fancily as Char had ever seen him dressed, except for his junior prom, when she and Beth, couple of pests that they'd been, had teased him and his buddy about looking like Laurel and Hardy.

I'm just being hyperobservant because I've got something to hide, Char rationalized, attempting to make herself feel better. It didn't work. There was that tingling in the backs of her knees again. Perhaps, she thought, if she simply admitted the obvious truth she'd get back to normal.

Adam Stiles was and always had been one hell of an attractive man.

There. She'd admitted it.

The problem was, she didn't pop back to normal. Instead she found herself looking at the tanned top of his hand as he shifted the car into gear.

"Did a crocodile bite off your hand, like Captain Hook?" Emily asked from the back seat.

Mortified, Char whipped around. "Emily!"

Adam laughed. "Nothing so exciting as that. I lost it in an accident at the sawmill."

"Oh. Yeah, I remember now."

Char didn't doubt her daughter for a moment. That had been a tense, dramatic, emotional day in Millbrook three years ago when Julian had raced to the hospital with his bloodied, mutilated brother. Attempts to sew his hand back on had failed. Adam Stiles, however, had never been one for brooding and self-pity; he'd gotten on with it. Char recalled hoping she'd have comparable courage should she ever face similar hardship, not that she'd expected she really would, at least not so soon.

While explaining the mechanics of his hook, which he was wearing less and less these days, Adam headed out to the restaurant in downtown Nashville that Char suggested. It wasn't the most expensive restaurant in the area, if only because she wanted a place at least somewhat child-oriented, for Emily's sake. The Stiles family had done very, very well for themselves in their two hundred years in southern Vermont. Adam could af-

ford to treat her and Em to dinner at any restaurant
Char might have chosen.

But, Char admitted, she would have preferred to
have treated *him*. That had been her plan when she and
Emily had moved to Tennessee: she was grabbing her
brass ring and off to make her fortune. Angling for free
dinners hadn't been a part of her dreams for her future.

"You okay?" Adam asked.

"Sure."

"You haven't said much."

"Is making conversation my responsibility?"

He scowled at her. "You know better."

"Let's just say I haven't seen anyone from Millbrook
in a year and it takes some getting used to and leave it
at that."

"Especially since that someone's me?"

There was no bitterness in his tone, no hint of self-
deprecation, just the simple understanding that he and
Char did know each other. His eyes half-closed, he
studied her a moment at a stoplight, his expression and
silence reminding her that this man was forty years old,
a widower, a father, the president of a profitable, highly
regarded family corporation. Adam Stiles was an intelligent, experienced man. He had been born, bred and
probably would die in Millbrook, Vermont, but in his
own way, he'd been around—and he knew people.
Char couldn't help wondering what Beth had told him
before he'd left for Nashville. Nothing, Char assured
herself. Beth didn't know enough to tell. *Remember
that. If Adam Stiles is my undoing, it's my own fault.
Right now he doesn't know anything.*

Finally she smiled, an easy, sincere smile that she
hoped pulled him off guard. "You're just being the
Adam Stiles I've known all my life."

The light turned green, and Adam redirected his attention to his driving. "I talked to Beth a little while ago. I told her the house you claimed you were living in is a museum."

"Did you offer to send her a brochure?" Char asked lightly.

Adam clamped his mouth shut.

"You have no sense of humor," Char said. "Beth does, I hope. The photograph I sent was a *joke*, Adam. Get it? A joke."

He didn't laugh or even crack a smile. "Okay, it was a joke. So where *do* you live?"

Char glanced at the back seat, where Emily was contentedly looking out the window. Having lived with this child for seven years, Char knew she was trying to catch as much of her mother's conversation as she possibly could. But Emily also knew better than to comment on her and her mother's current living quarters. The subject was verboten with anyone from Millbrook, particularly Adam Stiles. "Uncle" Adam, Char had explained to her wise-to-the-world daughter, just wouldn't understand.

"We have a place on the Cumberland River," Char replied smoothly. "It's a beautiful spot."

"And you have horses?"

"That's why I came down here."

Adam gave her a look that would have sliced anyone else in two, but Char merely yawned and settled back into her seat. Technically she had told the truth. No one had been more surprised than Adam when Millbrook's busiest hometown lawyer had announced she was off to central Tennessee to make her fortune—or at least fulfill a childhood dream—in horses. She had had the big city. She had had small-town New England. Now she wanted the rolling hills of Tennessee and the milder weather and the excitement of the New South. She and Beth used to fantasize about raising horses, owning land in Kentucky or Virginia, but it was the Nashville area that had captivated Char six years ago. She was visiting Beth and her now ex-husband on their incredible spread in central Tennessee, and Char had fallen in love with the area.

Just as a few cases had gone sour on her and Millbrook was beginning to seem smaller and smaller, Char's Great-Aunt Millicent had died, leaving her an unexpected inheritance. Horses and Tennessee seemed to be Char's destiny. So off she went. At the time she had thought she was making a sound, rational decision. Looking back, she realized she'd gone off on a whim—she'd seen that brass ring and gone for it. Maybe, though, that was how it should have been. Chasing dreams wasn't necessarily rational, and if she should have foreseen the nightmare her dream would become, then maybe the blinders and the faith were all a part of it, too. If she had paused to think, she might have stayed in Millbrook. And who knew but she might have landed in a bigger mess than she had by coming to Tennessee? Hard to imagine, but regrets were a bigger waste of time than dreams. Dreams you could do something about. Regrets you couldn't.

Adam, naturally, had paused to think on Char's account, but she had told him what she did with her life was none of his business. She could talk to Adam like that. Someone's being straight up with him had never cost him a night's sleep, Char was positive of that much. Always boringly rational and analytical, he had pointed out, quite unnecessarily, that she knew next to nothing about horses. Char had chosen not to make any attempt to justify her actions to him. He wasn't the most imaginative of men. She loved horses and had dreamed of raising Thoroughbreds since she was a kid. In her opinion that was enough analysis and all the rationale she needed.

"I'd like to see your place while I'm in town," he said.

Char felt ice cubes sliding down her back. There was no way she was going to invite Adam Stiles back to her tent! But she said, "Fine with me."

"Good. You can give me directions over dinner and I'll meet you there tomorrow. Are you free for lunch? My flight leaves a little before four."

"Lunch would be fine."

Less than twenty-four hours more of this man to go! Char stifled an urge to clap and cheer, even as she felt a pang of loneliness. What was wrong with her?

Lunch wouldn't be fine, of course, but she would deal with that in time. She ignored Adam's frank look of suspicion. She hadn't asked him to come to Tennessee and meddle in her life. That was his choice, and he'd have to bear the consequences. And it was fairly obvious that Beth hadn't called him off—or, if she'd tried, hadn't succeeded. Not that that would surprise Char. Adam Stiles had always been hardheaded and compulsive.

Well, she had until after dinner to come up with a way out of lunch. She had no intention of having Adam over to her particular spot on the Cumberland River. None.

They arrived at the restaurant Char had chosen, a good, solid steak house just beyond the country and western tourist traps. Even with one of her French braids starting to come apart, Emily looked great; Char had resurrected one of her old lawyer suits for herself.

With a scarf it didn't look too bad. She was confident Adam wouldn't remember it—not, she reminded herself, that she gave a damn if he did.

The restaurant was dark inside, with lots of wood and framed photographs of old Nashville, and they took a booth, Adam on one side, Char and Emily on the other. Char only had to glance at the menu, just to figure out which cut of steak she wanted. She directed Emily away from the mundane children's specials to the petite-sized sirloin tips, ignoring her persistent lobbying for a hot dog.

"You don't eat hot dogs in a place like this," Char told her. "People will think you're crude."

Emily scowled. "Then why are they on the menu?"

There was still plenty of no-nonsense Yankee left in her daughter, Char thought with a mother's mix of affection and annoyance. "To catch little girls not acting right. Order the steak. We'll have hot dogs tomorrow."

Adam had kept quiet during the exchange, apparently knowing better than to interfere in a mother-daughter discussion of dinner entrées. Char promised Emily she could pick out her choice of dessert, and that ended the matter. Steaks were ordered all around. Emily contemplated which dessert would be the biggest and sweetest and least appropriate as far as her mother was concerned.

The waiter delivered two beers, one for Adam, one for Char. Adam took a sip and leaned back comfortably. "So, if the photograph was just a joke, what were you doing out at Belle Meade this afternoon?"

"I do volunteer work there."

Char hated lying in front of Emily, but pride and survival were human impulses her daughter would come to understand at perhaps a younger age than most. And Em would figure out that with some people the truth was better off skirted.

Warming to her topic, Char went on. "Belle Meade was an internationally famous Thoroughbred nursery and stud in its day. Bonnie Scotland was born there."

"I'm not up on my horse history," Adam said dryly.

Char took a bigger drink of her beer than she'd intended, but welcomed the cold liquid in her throat. She was burning up under Adam's scrutiny! Why was he making her so damn nervous and self-conscious all of a sudden? She was known for her cool, had been for years. Beth had a hell of a nerve siccing her brother of all people onto someone she'd been friends with all her life. Never mind that Beth's motives were irreproachable and Char *had* invited trouble sending home that picture of Belle Meade. She didn't deserve having to outwit Adam Stiles. No one did.

"Bonnie Scotland was a top Thoroughbred of the nineteenth century," she went on, surprised at how relaxed she sounded. *And why not? You can handle Adam!* "Many of the most famous horses of the twentieth century are descendants of his, including Secretariat. You *have* heard of Secretariat?"

"Fastest Belmont Stakes ever run, Triple Crown winner, put out to stud until his death at nineteen last year." Adam obviously wasn't amused and gave her a look that told her so in no uncertain terms. "Don't be smug, Char. A year ago you didn't know a horse from a mule."

His remark wasn't, Char sadly knew, that much of an exaggeration. Unfortunately it still wasn't. As was her custom, however, she was learning—the hard way. She said, more defensively than she'd have liked, "I've wanted to have horses for as long as I can remember."

"Thoroughbreds?"

"Of course."

Adam contemplated his beer for a moment, slowly, deliberately, drawing his finger down the side of the frosted mug through the condensation. Something about his concentration and the movement of his finger struck Char as inordinately erotic. She was feeling hotter than ever, to the point of wanting to scoop ice out of her water glass and rub it over her face. But she resisted. How could she have explained? She was acting weird enough as it was.

He shifted his attention back to her. "Horses are an expensive hobby, aren't they?"

"They're not a hobby. They're what I do now."

To her relief Emily didn't counter her mother's claim. Char shot her a quick look, warning her to maintain her discreet silence on the touchy subject of what Mom did for a living.

"Ever miss lawyering?" Adam asked.

"With all your questions you should have been a lawyer yourself."

He grinned at her frank irritation. "You were born to argue, Ms. Bradford. Horses don't argue back. Can't be that much fun."

"People change."

"Not you, Char."

But he left it at that, with a glance at Emily, engrossed in her tropical fruit punch and studiously avoiding eye contact with either him or her mother. Char decided a change in subject was in order and suspected that Adam, a parent himself, would cooperate.

Swallowing her annoyance with him, she asked conversationally, "How's the mill?"

"Busy."

Talkative Adam. "Sorry I didn't make it up for Julian and Holly's wedding. Beth says they're quite a pair."

"I guess they deserve each other," he said with a laugh. "Holly sort of burst into Julian's life. Neither one'll ever be the same again, I don't think."

"Julian needed someone—he was turning into a recluse."

"He's happy. So's Holly. They're damn lucky and they know it." He smiled with sudden self-awareness. "But being a recluse isn't so awful."

"You should know. If it weren't for Abby and David, you'd be just as happy living in a cave."

He laughed. "Too dark."

"What about Beth? Is she seeing anyone special?"

"Nope. She's still smarting over her divorce, not that she'd ever admit it."

Beth's ex-husband, a man rich enough to consider horse breeding a pleasant hobby, was the *last* person Char wanted to talk about. She had had her own run-ins with Harlan Rockwood that Adam—and above all Beth—didn't need to know about.

"And you, Adam?"

"I've got too much work to do to be chasing women," he said casually. His eyes rested on her. "Someone interesting comes along, okay. If not, me and the kids are getting along just fine."

Mention of Abby and David sparked Emily's attention. "How're they doing?" she asked, obviously tired of being seen and not heard.

"Great," Adam said warmly. "They miss you."

Char resisted making a face. Adam was deliberately rubbing it in and they both knew it.

"Have you started making apple cider yet?"

"Some."

Cider making was a passion among the Stiles family, and Char once again felt the bite of nostalgia as Adam indulged her daughter with long, descriptive answers to her questions about cider, apple picking, pumpkins, the annual Columbus Day fair.

Autumn in New England...

As a kid, she'd taken the changing of the leaves for granted, giggling with Beth at the busloads of leaf-peepers. What was the big deal about Vermont's multicolored leaves? Tennessee was a beautiful state, as well. Char loved the rolling hills of the central basin and the long, lush springs. But her feelings about Vermont were mixed up with childhood and family and everything she'd left behind—house, office, law practice, the diner where she ate lunch, the woman at the library who used to help Emily pick out books. All of that was gone. She hadn't been in Tennessee long enough for it to be home yet. It would be, though, in time.

Although he had never really lived anywhere but Millbrook, did Adam ever get lonely? Did he ever long for his life to be something it wasn't? Char had never asked him. Such questions were too personal, too intimate. If nothing else, Adam might think she owed him answers to intimate questions in return. Like what the hell were she and Emily *really* doing in Tennessee?

Their steaks arrived, piping hot and utterly luscious, and conversation drifted to weather, food, schools. Ordinary, nonthreatening subjects. Char began to relax. The rich food and beer and light talk made her troubles seem less pressing and immediate, more distant. She found herself actually enjoying Adam's company. He seemed different on his own in Tennessee, where he was free from the pressures of being a

Millbrook Stiles, a single parent, a one-handed president of a highly regarded sawmill. Or perhaps it was just her. She supposed it didn't matter which. She was seeing a side of Adam—or looking at him—in a way she never had before. Before he had only been Beth's older brother. The hardworking, no-nonsense president of Mill Brook Post & Beam. Just Adam. Nothing more.

Now . . .

Oh, what do you know? He's still just Adam.

So why had she never really noticed the flecks of gray in his eyes? Why had she never really noticed the powerful muscles in his shoulders and the sun-bleached hairs on his wrist?

Why had she never wanted to touch him before?

She sat up straight. *Good Lord, I am going off the deep end!*

Clearing her throat, she made an effort to concentrate on her steak. She was at a vulnerable point in her life and Adam just happened to be there. He wasn't family, and he wasn't *exactly* a friend, but he knew her better than anyone else in the state of Tennessee did. And she knew him. He was familiar, if not comfortable. A part of the life she'd given up. *That* was why she was responding to him the way she was.

"Char?"

She looked up, startled, aware her thoughts had drifted and she hadn't been listening. "I'm sorry—what?"

"Nothing. It's not important. How's your dinner?"

"Wonderful."

She decided not to gush about what a treat dinner was. *It's come to this*, she realized miserably. *The high point in my week's going to be eating steak with Adam Stiles.*

Had she given up too much to chase rainbows and pots of gold? She bit back another assault of nostalgia, reminding herself that time and separation had a way of clouding the negative. Five minutes back in Millbrook and she'd be climbing the walls. She knew she would. *But maybe you shouldn't be worrying about Adam's loneliness. Maybe you should be worrying about your own.*

Later, she told herself. Right now just enjoy the food, the company, the memories.

Any regrets she might have had about dinner with Adam faded as she saw how much fun her daughter was having, how animated she was and thoroughly at ease with their hard-nosed Yankee friend from Vermont. True to the promise she'd made her mother that afternoon, Emily didn't bring up any forbidden subjects, namely anything, beyond the weather, related to their life in Tennessee.

To Char's surprise Adam went along with the lack of specifics. She assumed he either believed her claim of living in the Belle Meade mansion was a joke or he was just biding his time before he nailed her. Or maybe she was being silly and she should just tell him everything?

It was during dessert that he nailed her.

Char was treating her taste buds to a piece of warm pecan pie and watching Emily dive into a monstrous hot fudge sundae when Adam, calmly and without a word, slid a scrap of paper and a pencil across the table to her.

"Your address," he said.

There was nothing casual in his tone; he was steady, serious and wholly dubious. *So*, she thought, *he does think I'm hiding something!* It didn't matter that he was outsmarting her. Now who was being smug? She grabbed the pencil and without hesitation jotted down an address, even a map, and pushed it across to him.

"Lunch tomorrow," she said. "Noon's all right?"

"It's fine."

He was still suspicious. Char gave him her best cool smile. "Terrific."

He tucked the scrap of paper into a pocket. Char hid her victorious smile by taking a quick sip of coffee, but by the time Adam had dropped her back off at Belle Meade, she wasn't sure just what she'd won. She thanked him and agreed she'd see him tomorrow. Of course, she wouldn't. Not if he followed the directions she'd just given him.

"Tonight was nice," Adam said simply. He had gotten out of his car to open the passenger door for Emily, then, after giving her a quick good-night kiss, had come around to Char.

She couldn't bring herself to smile. "Yes," she said, her throat tight. "It was."

The way he was looking at her, she thought he might kiss her on the cheek or give her a hug or maybe just shake her hand. She even considered initiating something of the sort herself, but in the end they simply said good-night, got into their respective cars and left.

With Emily falling asleep on the seat beside her, Char drove back out toward the Cumberland River and thought of Adam and his soft laugh and his offer of friendship and wondered if she could be accused of cutting off her nose to spite her face. But, no, it wasn't friendship he had offered. She couldn't allow herself to be lured into that kind of thinking. She had a more important agenda to consider, anyway, like getting her life back in order. Beth was worried about her friend in Tennessee, and Adam Stiles was nothing if not the most conscientious of big brothers. He had wormed his way into Char's life out of duty to his sister, not out of concern for Char or anything so innocuous as friendship.

You're just unusually vulnerable, she told herself. _So you're more susceptible to friendly overtures. You don't really like Adam, remember?_

She remembered.

But what she didn't remember as she headed back to her so-called home was ever having felt so damn alone. The evening felt incomplete, and for the first time in her life, so did Char.

CHAR'S EYES and her voice hadn't matched.

The contradiction they had presented throughout a decidedly tantalizing dinner haunted Adam as he headed back to his hotel. Her eyes were deep and dark and filled with loneliness and determination and pain. They challenged him with unanswered questions and mysteries; they lured him with their pride and warmth—with the particular spirit that had always been a part of Charity Bradford.

Her voice, however, was all wiseacre Char, the smart, independent, cut-through-the-nonsense attorney who had given the citizens of Millbrook, Vermont, confidence that their legal interests were well represented. She had had her share of cases that had gone sour, particularly in the months before she'd absconded to Tennessee, but Char was tough. She could handle anything. _That_ was what her voice had said tonight.

Adam couldn't reconcile the two, the eyes and the voice. He had to wonder if Beth weren't right on target this time: something was going on with Char that she wasn't looking to admit to anyone.

She had always been stiff-necked, he reminded himself on his way to his room. He didn't recall her ever getting into anything she couldn't get herself out of or ever really needing his help or anyone else's. Being of an independent nature himself, he could understand her reluctance to bother anyone with needs she felt she ought to be able to meet on her own. Self-reliance ran hard and deep in both their souls.

He stuck his key into his hotel door. "She's a pain in the ass is what she is," he muttered, "and you're better off leaving her to her own devices."

She was a grown woman with a good education and the drive to succeed. She'd be fine without him sticking his nose in her life. After all, he had no right.

But as he undressed for bed, Adam kept seeing her eyes. Char was a family friend, and if she was too damn stubborn to admit she needed a hand . . .

With a sigh he got out his street map of the Nashville area and the scrap of paper with Char's directions to her *real* place. So where did she live? In something a bit smaller than the Belle Meade mansion, he was quite sure.

Then again, maybe not.

What erupted from his throat was a growl of unadulterated anger and frustration.

"That damn sneak!"

Her directions were easy to spot on the map because they pinpointed a place that had a red asterisk beside it, marking it as a tourist destination. It was called Cheekwood, an arts and botanical garden center at the edge of the Percy Warner Park, not far from the Belle Meade mansion.

There was a brochure in the desk in Adam's room. Cheekwood itself was, of course, a lovely mansion, currently open to the public.

Adam crumpled up the scrap and wished Char were here so that he could suggest what she should do with it. Then he recalled the sparkle that had suddenly appeared in her eyes after she'd jotted down her directions. He could see her looking out at him over the rim of her coffee cup, her dark eyes so filled with life and energy he'd had to catch his breath. Why the hell hadn't he noticed until now what a vibrant, sexy woman she was? He'd thought, stupidly he now realized, that maybe she was more pleased to have him coming to lunch than he'd anticipated, that maybe—just maybe— Beth was overreacting to her friend's mysterious behavior.

Naturally he'd been wrong. He usually was where Char was concerned.

The sparkle in her eyes had been nothing but a smart-assed woman relishing her victory.

Cheekwood.

He'd been had again.

"One round to you, Char," he said. For the next one he would damn well be ready.

THE NEXT MORNING Char awoke in a state of confusion and anxiety, with a mood to match. Her daughter didn't help by being inordinately cheerful. She pranced and chattered and giggled her way into the car, not letting up even as they approached her elementary school. School started earlier in Tennessee than in Vermont, something Emily didn't necessarily appreciate. She had commented that Abby and David Stiles were still enjoying their summer vacation while *she* was sitting behind a desk. Char had pointed out that an early start meant an early release and Em had been on summer vacation in May while her friends in Vermont were still in school.

"Do you think Uncle Adam will bring Abby and David to Tennessee sometime?" she asked.

"He might," Char replied judiciously. She hoped to hell not. She would like to show Adam's kids around Nashville, but not anytime soon. Later, when she had straightened out her life.

Emily wasn't easily distracted from something she wanted. "I'll ask him when he comes to lunch. He'll still be there when I get out of school, right?"

"Em . . ."

"I can show him the river. You going to make dessert, Mom? That sundae was *sooooo* good last night."

"Em, Adam won't be coming for lunch."

Her face fell. "He won't? How come?"

"Because."

"*Mom.*"

Char sighed. "Because I don't want him to see where we live. He'll get the wrong impression. You know and I know it's just temporary, but he might not think so. Then he'll go back to Millbrook and tell everybody, and I hate gossip. So he's not coming to lunch. Even if he did, he'd have to leave before you got home. He's flying back to Vermont today."

"Can I send him a postcard?"

"Of course you can."

Emily had developed a zest for sending everyone she knew postcards; they kept her in touch with friends and relatives up north. Satisfied, she kissed her mother goodbye and trotted into school, her life, as far as she was concerned, nothing less than delightful. There were moments when that was Char's only consolation.

She headed toward Belle Meade and the part-time job that had kept her sane and relatively on her feet in the past weeks. She was looking into taking the Tennessee bar—even into decent-paying legal jobs she could do while waiting to pass the bar. It wasn't what she had in mind when she'd left Vermont a year ago, but better than starving. And the adventure had gone out of camping out in a tent.

"You've really made a mess of things, haven't you?" she asked her reflection in the rearview mirror.

Her reflection didn't answer. It didn't need to. In her eyes she could see that the dream that had brought her to central Tennessee had turned into a nightmare. But it was a nightmare of her own making, and she would see herself through it, alone.

ADAM HAD CHANGED rented cars and parked the new one, even more nondescript than the previous one, just below the Belle Meade exit. There was no way Char could leave without his seeing her. Until then he'd just wait, private eye style.

She left at noon. Adam was sweating and hungry and impatient as hell, but he forced himself not to drive up on her bumper. With the engine on, at least he could turn up the air-conditioning to high. He felt the cool air as he dropped in a couple of cars behind her, smooth and easy.

Cheekwood, he thought with a grunt of disgust. He hadn't even bothered to call Beth and tell her. He'd get to the bottom of this one himself.

Not going anywhere near Percy Warner Park or Cheekwood, Char's battered vehicle hit I-40, the east-west interstate, heading east. Adam stayed as far back as he dared. He wasn't going to lose her. His gas tank was full. He could follow her to Chattanooga if that was where she was going. It didn't make any difference to him. She'd tried to lead him on another wild-goose chase, and joke or not, he wasn't amused.

This is crazy, man. You and Charity Bradford have never gotten along, will never get along, and she's made it damn clear she wants you to get the hell out of Tennessee and leave her alone.

But he thought of her eyes, warm and troubled, and inhaled deeply, undeterred.

He put his rented car into cruise control and decided he might as well relax. Crazy or not, he was determined to find out what was going on with Ms. Charity Winnifred. And, if need be, he'd catch a different flight home. His kids were safe with Julian and Holly and the mill would do just fine without him. He would have to get back, of course, but for now he wasn't in any hurry.

3

WHEN SHE PULLED into the parking lot of a squat brick building on an overbuilt highway west of Nashville, Char tried to keep her spirits from sinking. She told herself appearances could be deceiving. The large, overflowing trash bin didn't have to mean anything. Neither did the potholed asphalt or strip of dead, unmown grass that served as a border between the parking lot and the highway. She tried not to let the building's dingy trim or the tacky venetian blinds in its dusty picture windows dishearten her. People had to get their start somewhere. Not everyone could go straight from law school into a prestigious law firm in a historic building, with tasteful furnishings and private parking. Just because she had didn't mean she didn't believe in roadside lawyers.

But as she climbed out of her car, taking care to lock it up tight, she had to acknowledge a slight sagging of her shoulders, a pronounced wrenching of her insides...and a certain relief that Adam Stiles was on his way to Cheekwood for lunch instead of here with her now. How could she expect him to understand the predicament she'd gotten herself into? Even she didn't understand it.

Bracing herself, she made her way to the office of Mr. Howard Marston, attorney-at-law.

The office consisted of two small rooms, both smoke-filled, both cheaply furnished, neither what Char

would call spotless. Again she reminded herself that
people had to start somewhere. There was no one
seated at the gray metal desk in the outer office, but
Char could see through the opened door to the inner
office, where a man, probably around her age, was
twisting a rubber band around a pencil while he listened on the phone. He was a tall, fair man dressed in
the low-priced version of what he obviously considered a high-priced attorney ought to wear, right down
to the horn-rimmed glasses.

He motioned for Char to come in. She did so.

"Got that?" he said to the party on the other end of
the phone. "Great. Be there in twenty minutes." He
hung up and gave a long-suffering shake of the head.
"Can't even order a barbecue sandwich without listening to somebody's sob story. Everyone wants free legal
advice, you know?"

Char decided she ought to smile. After several weeks
of pounding the pavement, she'd discovered her off-
hand remarks had an unfortunate tendency to irritate
her interviewers. Best to keep her mouth shut. Adam
would say that went against her nature, but—

She cut herself off at once. *Why* did she keep thinking about Adam Stiles?

"I'm Charity Bradford," she said, trying not to sound
arrogant, timid, coy or overconfident, just matter-of-
fact.

"Right, right." He rose and reached across his cluttered desk to shake her hand. "Have a seat, have a seat."

Char wondered if he was going to say everything
twice as she eased down onto an orange plastic chair.
Her eyes drifted to the framed degrees on the mud-
colored wall behind Howard Marston. He'd graduated
from a two-bit law school in Ohio. Fine, she thought.

Some of the most practical, down-to-earth lawyers she knew had attended less-than-prestigious law schools. She was glad, however, she had left off her own Columbia law degree from her résumé, not to mentioned Wellesley College and her Park Avenue law firm experience. So far they hadn't gotten her anywhere with the kind of jobs she could get, not having taken the Tennessee bar.

"So you're a newcomer to Nashville?"

"Yes. It's a lovely area."

"Too darn hot in the summer for my taste. I'd love to get back to Ohio myself, but I got a pretty good business percolating here." He tapped out a cigarette, peering at a copy of her doctored résumé. "So you've worked for a lawyer before?"

"Yes, sir. I was a paralegal for Elizabeth Stiles in Millbrook, Vermont, for five years."

Char marveled at the steadiness of her voice, but she'd always been a better liar than Beth, who wouldn't have taken to being fictionalized as a lawyer. She had an altogether too-typical view of lawyers as leeches with legs and tassel loafers. After ten years, during which she'd never owned a pair of tassel loafers, Char had quit trying to disabuse her best friend of her unflattering stereotype and settled for Beth's grudging admission that Char was the exception to the rule.

Howard Marston pushed his cheap horn-rimmed glasses higher on his nose. "I don't guess you did much corporate work up in Millbrook, Vermont."

And I don't guess you do much down here, Char thought, not liking his smug tone. She had, of course, done a great deal of corporate work in New York City. She said judiciously, "A number of Ms. Stiles's clients are small businesses."

He lit his cigarette, exhaled a cloud of smoke and smiled condescendingly. "I'm sure."

Char bristled at his implicit put-down of Millbrook. But why should she want to defend a town she had spent most of her life wanting to leave? Millbrook was probably just the kind of place Howard Marston thought it was. Still, she *knew* what Millbrook was. He was just assuming.

"You've come south for greater opportunities?" Marston asked.

Yeah, Char thought, like living in a tent and trying to get a job with a man who doesn't even have the courtesy to ask me if I mind if he smokes. She gritted her teeth. "You could say that, yes."

"All right, then, let's go over your skills."

They did so in painstaking detail. Char vowed she would never again take paralegals or any kind of office help for granted. She had never thought she had acted superior and knew she had never *felt* superior, but after weeks on the other side of the lawyer's desk, she had begun to squirm at memories of the rare occasions when pressure and a packed schedule had gotten to her and she'd bitten off the nearest head. Never again.

As Marston rattled on, Char began to gather he expected her to work for pittance, with no compensation for overtime, and serve as a combination secretary, receptionist, gofer and paralegal.

Finally he settled back in his leather-look chair. "I assume you're still interested?"

Char had launched herself to the edge of her chair and was about to nail him with a pointed lecture, but she remembered her daughter. The job was for Emily. They couldn't go on living in a tent. They had to have a place to live, clothes, food. After their night out on the town with Adam, Emily had taken less kindly than usual to pulling slugs out of her sneakers that morning. As the saying went, the thrill of outdoor living was gone. Mama had to get herself back on her feet, and fast.

She said of course she was still interested.

And Howard Marston said he wanted her to take a typing test.

"A what?"

"We have a personal computer and a memory typewriter." He handed her what looked to be the nastiest legal document he could lay his hands on; a good legal secretary could dash it off in a few minutes. Char would need half a day. Marston gestured to the outer office. "Take your pick."

Death by hanging or death by electrocution. Char asked, "What percentage of this job is typing?"

"That all depends on how fast you type. I'd estimate sixty percent."

Char frowned. "That's not the job you advertised, Mr. Marston."

"I beg your pardon?"

As soon as she could afford to in her practice in Millbrook, Char had hired a full-time legal secretary. She had assumed Marston already had one and she would be a paralegal, as he'd stated he wanted. She might be able to fake it for the moment and get the job. But how long before he discovered her inadequacies and fired her? She had to get her credentials in order and hang out her own shingle. It'd be back to lawyering—back to Go—but at least she wouldn't lie awake nights wondering what kind of nut-case mother she was to her poor kid.

She took the typing test and flunked.

On her way out Howard Marston balled up her résumé and arced it into his wastebasket across the room, no doubt his entertainment for the day.

Char slunk back to her car and almost wished she hadn't given Adam false directions to her place. They could have grilled catfish and drunk lemonade on the big rock overlooking the Cumberland River in front of her tent.

And I could have listened to him badger me about how the hell I ended up living like Huck Finn.

No thanks.

She pulled out of the parking lot and saw but paid no attention to the nondescript sedan that edged in behind her.

Twenty minutes later she realized the nondescript sedan was following her. Had she not been so preoccupied with her problems she would have realized it sooner. Now she had already made the turn off the main road onto the back road that led to her spot on the river. But the creepy feeling that raised the hairs at the back of her neck quickly dissipated, replaced by something a little too close to exhilaration for her tastes.

Adam.

He was in the sedan. *He* was following her.

"Thinks he's hot stuff, I'll bet," she muttered, glancing in her rearview mirror. The sun was at such an angle that she couldn't see his face, but the driver had to be Adam.

She bit down on the corner of her mouth. What was she going to tell him? She was on a picnic. Or off fishing. Adam being Adam, he'd demand to see her picnic basket or her fishing rod, neither of which she had on her.

She'd just have to tell him the truth.

Sort of.

IN THE HOT, still afternoon air the Cumberland River flowed quietly through the hills of central Tennessee, so different from the bright, cold Mill Brook rushing down from the mountains of southern Vermont. Adam slid his rented car to a stop behind Char's beat-up hatchback. More than once on the narrow back road he had wondered if she'd spotted him and was leading him on yet another wild-goose chase. Belle Meade, Cheekwood. Was there another museum tucked away out here?

He rolled down his window and waited for her to stomp over to him. He figured he'd catch it now, but she surprised him with her bright smile. "So you found me."

Adam leaned back and studied her for a moment, aware of a sudden increase in his heart rate as she came closer. Pure aggravation, no doubt. Char had a knack for bringing out the worst in him. The heat had settled her blouse against the soft contours of her breasts and abdomen and added a sheen to her skin, a frizz to her hair. She looked more human than he had ever noticed before . . . more beautiful.

"You're not funny, Char," he told her. "You never have been."

Her eyes narrowed slightly, an echo of the sharp lawyer so many residents of Millbrook had counted on. She tried her bright, airy, guiltless smile again. "You're mad about Cheekwood, aren't you? Oh, Adam, don't be so serious!"

"I'm not mad. I just want to know what you're hiding."

"Nothing. Don't you get it? Cheekwood was—"

"A joke?" He could feel himself reddening, could feel his heart thudding in his chest. For a nickel he'd jump out of the damn car and . . . *and what?* Best not carry that thought too far, he decided. He was, after all, a prudent man. "Gee, Char, add the picture of Belle Meade you sent Beth and that makes two jokes in one year. That has to be a record for a no-nonsense lawyer such as yourself. Even when you were twelve you used to get disgusted when other kids played practical jokes. Remember what they used to call you?"

The feigned smile disappeared. "I remember."

"Acid Mouth," he said. "Acid Mouth Bradford."

"Do you remember *everything?* People change, Adam. *I've* changed. Coming to Tennessee and getting out of the legal profession has lightened me up. I've discovered I have a sense of humor."

"No, you don't, Char. Even if Belle Meade and Cheekwood were your idea of jokes, that proves you have a long way to go before anyone'll start calling you for Johnny Carson. But I don't believe they were jokes. I believe they were your attempt to pull one over on Beth and myself."

"You're the one with no sense of humor," Char snapped, pulling open his car door. "Since you're here you might as well have a look around."

Just what he was having a look around at, Adam wasn't sure. He climbed out of the car, shutting the door softly behind him, as he noticed how stiff and tense Char was. That wasn't like the Charity Winnifred Bradford he knew. Her incomparable blend of cool and irascibility had always pulled her through a confrontation with any hard-nosed judge, any hysterical client, any crisis of her own or someone else's doing. For all her griping about life in southern Vermont, Char, if hardly ever predictable, had always been solid and reliable.

Until now.

"Living in a tent these days?" he asked in as neutral a tone as he could manage.

She shrugged. "I suppose that's what it looks like."

It certainly did. A large tent was set up on a picturesque knoll above the river in a grassy area surrounded by birch, small oak, poplar and cedar trees. There was a grill set up out front, with a small, weather-beaten picnic table, Emily's bicycle, a couple of Adirondack chairs painted dark green. The place did have a certain homey charm. But it wasn't Belle Meade, it wasn't Cheekwood and it presented more questions than it answered.

Char, however, wasn't saying anything, just standing beside him with her arms crossed tightly over her chest. Adam didn't blame her for keeping quiet. She had already dug her hole plenty deep enough. And even when he *was* in a good mood, Adam knew he didn't much look it, and right now he was far, far from being in a good mood.

He had to unclench his jaw to speak. "What do you do, catch fish for supper?"

"As often as I can, yes. Emily loves fish." Char squinted up at him, unrepentant if still tense. "Me and Huck Finn."

"Huck Finn didn't have a seven-year-old daughter."

"I take damn good care of Emily."

"Does she do her homework by flashlight?"

"She does her homework before it gets dark—and she's just seven. She doesn't get much homework."

Adam wasn't impressed. "Does she brush her teeth in the river?"

Char's expression hardened. "I don't have to explain myself to you, Adam. But, as it happens, we have bottled water in the tent and a battery-operated light."

Frowning, Adam walked over to a large rock on the edge of the knoll, overlooking the slow-moving river. His traitorous mind conjured an image of sitting there with Char, watching the sunset while Emily and his kids ran around and climbed trees.

"What about snakes?" he asked.

"We're trying to catch a water moccasin for a pet," Char said sarcastically behind him, "maybe cook one up for supper one night."

"Damn it, Char." Adam tried to bite off his anger, but swung around at her. "What the hell's wrong with you? You lie to your friends. You're raising your daughter in a tent. You don't have a job to speak of. What did you do, blow all your money on a horse?"

"My life," she said, slowly and very clearly, "is none of your business."

Adam wasn't buying it, not this time. "Beth is my sister and your best friend. She's worried about you. Doesn't that mean anything to you?"

Char just tightened her lips and didn't say a word.

Adam wasn't in the mood to back off. "A lot of people in Millbrook would love to have you back as their lawyer. You've got friends in Vermont, people who care about you and would be glad to help you get back on your feet. You wouldn't even have to swallow your pride and ask for help. They'd just be there for you."

"Adam," Char said with surprising patience.

"What the hell are you going to do come winter?" he demanded, on a roll now. "Tennessee may not get as cold as Vermont, but it gets cold enough to make living in a tent uncomfortable, especially for a kid." He exhaled in frustration and raked his hand through his hair. "Hell. If I have to, Char, I'll haul your ass back to Vermont myself."

"Adam—"

"I mean it. I'm not going to stand back and let you—"

"*Adam!* Will you please shut up and listen to me?" Char had raised her voice to a shout, but lowered it now that she had his attention. She sighed, uncrossing her arms. "I appreciate your concern. Really, I do. I know Beth had you check up on me, and you've got better things to do with your time than meddle in my life on your sister's behalf. And I haven't exactly been fair to you. I see that now. I've been having some fun with you, apparently somewhat at my expense as well as yours."

Adam eyed her suspiciously, refusing to be taken in by her dark, honest eyes or the softness of her mouth. She had always been able to outlie Beth. He said, "Go on."

She took a deep breath. "You see, the tent's temporary. Emily and I are doing an experiment. Living on the river like this is a learning experience—for both of us, actually. We're learning about subsistence living, fishing, rivers, wildlife, weather. You wouldn't believe all the birds we've seen, how good a time we've had without so much...I don't know, so much *stuff* around us."

Her dark eyes angled toward Adam, ever so slightly, and the pink tip of her tongue dragged across her lower lip, which looked parched. Lying, he figured, must dry out the system.

When he didn't say anything, she climbed up on the big rock overlooking the river and went on. "I want Emily to appreciate the world around her and to know she can survive—*thrive*—without tons and tons, literally, of material possessions. We've been living a pretty stark existence, I admit, but it's been terrific. We've learned to appreciate what's important."

Her voice took on a wistfulness, an unexpected sincerity, that drew Adam closer, made him want to get inside this woman's head and find out what was really going on. Something profound had happened to Charity Bradford in the past year. Before leaving her beautiful hometown in the hills of southern Vermont, she had been known for her brutally realistic view of small-town life, which she refused to romanticize.

Adam joined her on the rock. "And what's that, Char? What's important?"

She didn't look at him, but kept her eyes fixed on the river. "Each other, our dreams, our place in the world, not as users, but as givers. That sounds sappy, I know, but right now a beautiful sunset pleases me more than— I don't know, than anything I've ever owned. And the chance to appreciate that sunset counts for something, too. I'm not just running around and chasing pots of gold any longer. I believe in hard work, but I guess being out here has made me redefine my definition of success. I hope it has for Emily, as well. I want her to be practical, I want her to develop skills and the drive that will see her through life. But I think now we both see that we need to have our own yardsticks for success and not allow ourselves to be tricked into using someone else's."

She stopped suddenly and looked around at Adam, her eyes wide and her cheeks flushed. "I haven't yapped that much about anything in ages," she said, and laughed, a little embarrassed. "Must be the heat. Would you like something to drink?"

Adam shook his head, forcing himself to pull his gaze from the haunting depths of her eyes. Maybe the setting was getting to him, as well. "No, thanks. If the tent's just you being weird, you must have a regular place to live. Where?"

Her eyes narrowed immediately, taking on the incisiveness that had made her a lawyer people wanted on their side. "You want to see my house?"

"And meet Em's Peruvian nanny."

"You don't trust me."

He looked her straight in the eye. "Not a lick."

She jumped down off the rock, and Adam followed, landing closer to her than he would have liked. "Adam, I'm what you might call a lady farmer. I hire people to do the work on my place while I do other things. I'm sorry if I've led you to believe anything else."

"Your horse venture's been a success, then?"

"Of course."

"What were you doing at that sleazy lawyer's office?"

"Don't get prosecutorial with me, Adam. But, as it happens, that was a wild-goose chase *I* was sent on. I'd heard this guy had a top colt for sale and thought I'd check it out. You have to act fast in this business, chase down every lead. If I'd known my way around Nashville better, I'd have realized I was just going to waste my time, which I certainly did."

Adam didn't say a word, just studied the woman who had been his sister's best buddy forever and wondered if he could believe anything she was telling him. He didn't think so.

"Look, speaking of time, I have to run and pick up Emily. If you want to see my house, all you have to do is follow this road back to the fork, bear left, and it'll take you right up to the main house. I'm actually on my own land here."

"Then you do have a house?"

"Uh-huh. It was a steal, Adam. The guy who owned it went bankrupt, and there I was with cash in my hand. It's not Belle Meade or Cheekwood, but it's close enough for my tastes. You don't have to bother checking it out if you don't have time. I know you have a flight to catch."

"I can catch another. In fact, why don't you bring Emily up to the house and we can talk more. Better yet, I'll go with you to pick her up."

"That's not necessary."

Her tone was cool. Too cool. Adam said, "Char, if this is another lie . . ."

She laughed, the coolness vanishing as quickly as it had appeared. "I have had fun with you, Adam, and I'm sorry if I worried you. I just didn't realize you'd get so carried away with my supposed problems. I mean, how could you ever think I'd be reduced to living in a tent?"

She had a point there. Adam didn't know whether he should squirm for having jumped to entirely wrong conclusions about her fate in Tennessee or pick her up and dunk her in the river until she finally told him the truth.

Was she lying or wasn't she?

"Adam," she said gently, taking his hand, "have you ever known me to fail at anything?"

In truth, he hadn't. "There's always a first time, Char."

"This isn't it, not for me."

With that, she headed off to her car, but Adam stayed put, watching how stiffly she moved. Something still wasn't right. "Is that heap you drive part of your anti-materialism kick?"

She whirled around at him, all hair and eyes and beautiful mouth. "Couldn't have said it better myself. Left at the fork, Adam. See you in about twenty minutes. Oh—the housekeeper's name is Ginger."

"Ginger," he repeated, but Char was already in her car, revving up the engine.

A housekeeper named Ginger, a Peruvian nanny, a big spread on the Cumberland River. It could all be true.

Then again, with Char, you just never knew.

Deciding he'd never get away with trying to follow her again, Adam got into his rented car. Left at the fork. Well, why not? If there was no housekeeper named Ginger, no Peruvian nanny, no big spread, he knew where to find Char.

And find her he would. He was damn sick of her lies...and altogether too intrigued by her eyes. He would deal with the lies now. The eyes...

It was hot in Tennessee, he was away from his kids, away from his work. His response to those dark, mesmerizing eyes had nothing to do with Charity Bradford and would cure itself within hours of being back at the mill.

He shook his head and started up the car. Now who was lying?

First things first. He sped off, kicking up dust behind him. Left at the fork. Ginger. Back in twenty minutes.

"You'd better hope it's so, Char," he muttered. "You'd better hope it's so."

4

CHAR'S HEART WAS POUNDING, her shirt sticking to her as she waited behind an abandoned shack in a turnaround off the back road to her camp on the river. She had turned off her car engine but hadn't bothered rolling down the windows. Before she could suffocate, Adam's rented car puttered past her.

She collapsed over the steering wheel in relief: she would get through this mess. All of it, not just the fleeting irritation Adam presented. In the end she would triumph. She just knew it. If she had any doubt, she didn't know if she could keep on. She would just give up and return to Millbrook in defeat.

If only she could figure out what was going on with her. All these lies, all this posturing. She was playing games with Adam Stiles and she wasn't a game player.

She rolled down her window and listened.

Nothing.

Adam was on his way. Within minutes he'd turn left at the fork and that would be that. He would be out of her life for good. Henceforth he would have nothing—absolutely nothing—to do with her.

She couldn't think about that now. Shifting her car into gear, she doubled back to her campsite.

Maybe what she was doing with Adam Stiles wasn't playing games. Maybe, she thought miserably, all she was doing was saving face. But wasn't that all she had left?

She left the engine running when she jumped out of her car. She worked fast, breathlessly, sloppily. She dragged everything out of her tent, pulled up stakes, folded, jammed, stuffed and otherwise forced as much as she could into her hatchback. What didn't fit into the hatch, she shoved into the back and front seats. What didn't fit anywhere—the grill, the Adirondack chairs—she left.

She was sobbing when she finished. She blamed the heat and overexertion and panic and even too much red meat last night for supper. She blamed Adam's relentless nature and told herself she was glad to be rid of him. Damn glad. Smart thinking, sending him off as she had.

But she kept sobbing, smearing dirt and tears and sweat over her face with the backs of her hands.

She hadn't cried in years. Not even when Aunt Millicent had died. Dear Aunt Millie. Her death had been the catalyst for her grandniece's move to Tennessee. What would she have to say now? Something, for sure. Aunt Millie had always had something to say.

I've got to calm down, Char thought. *I'll go out for coffee and biscuits and think about where I'm going to set up housekeeping next. We'll be fine, Emily and I.*

She pictured the farm of her dreams, she pictured Millbrook Center and Old Millbrook Common and her little eighteenth-century house and her office in the village with the window boxes of petunias. For the holidays she and Em would pick princess pine and cut white pine boughs and arrange them in the boxes with pinecones.

She pictured their wood stove on cold nights, pictured running water and flush toilets and their refrigerator with its place for eggs and their stove with four burners and their washing machine.

She smelled cracked wheat bread baking in the oven and heard Emily roller skating in the living room with friends . . . and she saw a gray-faced Adam Stiles standing in the doorway telling her his wife was dead and he needed her help. She was his attorney and maybe his friend.

He hadn't been afraid to ask for her help.

Char pictured it all—Millbrook, dreams, memories, fantasy, reality, the day they had buried her Great-Aunt Millicent who had left Char so much money and told her to go for broke in life, if that was what she wanted. *Don't be afraid to chase rainbows.* Char pictured all she'd had, all she'd given up.

What she had left was nothing.

Except Emily.

"Thank God," she whispered, wiping her face with a tissue and disgusted because she was being a damn fool. She had her daughter and her own strength of character and skills and education. She hadn't lost anything important.

What did you do, blow all your money on a horse?

Good ol' Adam. He did know how to hit a nail on the head. It was just as well, she decided as she banged her car into gear, that she had sent him off on yet another wild-goose chase.

THE WINDING BACK ROAD was deceptive, for the place Char had sent Adam to easily rivaled Belle Meade or Cheekwood. The paved driveway was flanked by mature cedar trees, beyond which were rolling pastures and the Cumberland River, shimmering in the late-afternoon heat. At the end of the driveway stood a spectacular Greek Revival house, as beautifully landscaped as any museum, with stables and outbuildings in stone. Adam half expected to see a sign directing him to the visitor's parking lot, but the knot in his stomach told him this was no museum.

Neither, he felt certain, was it Char's place. A private residence perhaps, but not hers, no matter how good her nose for a deal. Millicent hadn't left her *that* much money. And this place had about it the look of tradition and family, the kind of property handed down from generation to generation. Adam wouldn't have been surprised if it had never been up for sale, never mind bought by a Vermont Yankee. He wished he had Beth with him. She knew all the well-to-do in central Tennessee from her brief marriage to Harlan Rockwood. Wildly busy himself during those years, Adam had never had a chance to visit her and Harlan.

He parked in the driveway and headed down a trim brick walkway to the columned porch and the front door, where he rang the doorbell. God only knew who would answer, but he'd bet it wouldn't be a housekeeper named Ginger.

He was wrong.

Ginger was a plain, older woman with a strong central Tennessee accent. Her manner was polite and amiable, but she kept Adam out on the porch. "How can I help you?"

"I'm a friend of Charity Bradford's."

"Oh?"

"She's supposed to meet me back here."

"Mr. . . . ?"

"Stiles," he supplied, "Adam Stiles. I'm from Vermont."

Ginger took a breath and held it, her expression telling Adam she had opinions she was trying to keep to herself. Finally she said, "Miss Bradford isn't here."

"I know. She's gone to pick up her daughter. She'll be back—"

"I don't think so."

Ginger had crossed her arms and was shaking her head, looking a bit sad. Adam frowned. "This isn't Char's house, is it?"

"No, I'm afraid it isn't."

"Mind if I ask whose house it is?"

That was a question Ginger could answer with pride. "This house belongs to Mr. Harlan Rockwood."

IN ADDITION TO ALL her other falsities, Char had lied to Adam about when she had to pick up her daughter. She'd had two more hours before she had to be at the school. During that time she accomplished a great deal, including unloading her car. She hadn't given in, not to guilt, not to anger, not to depression, not to exhaustion. She would get through this disaster. She had, after all, no other choice.

Emily, ever her perky self, jumped into the car and yanked the door shut. "Did Uncle Adam leave?"

The sight of her daughter's eyes, so huge in the confines of the car, made Char's stomach lurch. What a life she was forcing Em to live! How could she do it? *Because you have to.* But did she? Couldn't she swallow her pride and go back to Vermont? She tried to tell herself it wasn't just a matter of pride, but also of doing what was right, what had to be done. Maybe she was kidding herself. Maybe Adam was right.

"Yes," she said. "He had to get back and see Abby and David."

Emily pushed her sweaty bangs off her forehead. "Think he'll come back?"

"He might. You never know with Adam."

If I were him, I'd never want to see me again. Char gripped the steering wheel, wishing that thought didn't make her feel so damn desolate. She had no idea why it did. Months used to go by without her giving any thought whatsoever to Adam Stiles. He was sort of like a big old rock in the woods, always there, never changing. Now Char was wondering if she'd ever stop thinking about the man.

"How was your day?" she asked her daughter.

Emily rattled on for a few minutes about gross school lunches, the third-graders who thought they were so cool, the real neat bug experiment they were doing in class and the journals she and the rest of her classmates were keeping. Emily's spelling wasn't the best and her punctuation nonexistent, but she loved telling "Ira"— the name of the fictional person she wrote to in her journal—about the goings-on in her life. Char had had to force herself to respect her daughter's privacy and not snoop. Not that Emily cared. What she didn't read aloud to her mother she told her.

But not today. Whatever she'd written in her journal today she wasn't going to tell one poor tired mother.

"Why not?" Char asked.

"Because it's private."

"What does a seven-year-old know about private?"

Emily clamped her mouth shut and that, Char could tell, was that. Not that she was willing to give up just yet. "You complained about me not letting you have a hot dog last night, didn't you?"

Emily shot her mother a look that made Char remember both the kid's parents were lawyers.

"Well, I don't care," Char said. "Hot dogs are made out of pig lips and—"

"Mom!" Emily giggled. "Hot dogs aren't made out of pig lips."

"Have you ever considered what they *are* made out of?"

"Cereal."

"Cereal? Where'd you hear that?"

"On a commercial."

"We don't have a TV."

"When we were in Vermont. I remember. Come on, Mom. I know hot dogs aren't made out of pig lips. And they're not made out of dogs, either. I used to think that when I was little."

"Then why are they called dogs? They don't look like dogs."

"That'd be gross."

"True," Char conceded. "So what did you say about your mother in your journal?" But Emily buttoned up, and Char laughed. "You don't have to tell me. Honestly. I can see a reporter trying to get information out of you if you ever become a lawyer."

"No way. I'm going to be an archaeologist."

"When I was seven I wanted to become a pirate and sail the seven seas." And when she was eight, and from then on, she had wanted to own horses and have space and rolling hills around her. Ah, well. She patted Emily on the knee. "Guess what? I have a surprise for you."

Emily rubbed her hands together in instant excitement. "Uncle Adam stayed?"

Char shook her head, forcing herself not to feel guilty over Emily's obvious longing for the connection to her past that Adam represented. Kids were adaptable, and Emily a free-spirited, gutsy one at that, but Vermont to her was still home. She had friends in Tennessee, but the roots hadn't sunk in deep yet.

"No, Emily, Adam was just visiting. He had to go home to be with his kids. We'll go back to Millbrook someday and visit, okay? Anyway, my surprise is better than having Uncle Adam take us out for another night on the town."

Emily was dubious about that. "It is?"

"Sure. Close your eyes."

In a few minutes Char parked along the curb in front of a tiny Craftsman-style cottage in a small town west of Nashville, where rents weren't as high as downtown and Emily wouldn't have to switch schools. Nevertheless, the security deposit and first month's rent had cost Char every cent—and more—that she had saved. She'd had to dip into her fund to repay Beth Stiles the money she had given Char to invest in her Tennessee horse project. What had become Char's nightmare was still Beth's dream, and Char was determined her best friend would get back every penny she had entrusted to her. Dipping into money she didn't consider her own bothered Char, but continuing to live in a tent when the adventure for her and Emily was long past didn't just bother her. It was eating away at her insides. She didn't have next month's rent, but that was thirty days away.

"Open your eyes," she said softly. Then she smiled. "Welcome home, kiddo."

Emily squealed and threw her arms around her mother's neck, and all Char had endured in the past twenty-four hours suddenly seemed inconsequential—even worth it. They examined the cottage together. There was only one bedroom, which Emily would get, plus a small living room, an eat-in kitchen and an old-fashioned bathroom with water stains in the tub, but after their tent the little house seemed like a palace. Emily especially loved the postage-stamp backyard dominated by a huge pecan tree. She couldn't wait to hang her bird feeder. The question of furniture was secondary in the minds of both mother and daughter. Their cottage was clean and dry, and they could bake cookies tonight and have a hot shower in the morning.

Silently Char thanked Adam Stiles for forcing her off that river.

That night she and Emily had stuffed pasta shells and salad and for dessert, baked oatmeal cookies. Emily went to her cot a happy child. Sitting up in her unfurnished living room, Char listened to the rain sweeping through central Tennessee and for the first time in months felt satisfied, if so damn alone. Today a house, tomorrow groceries, the next day—who knows? A table? Curtains?

She did have a future.

And that future included settling a score with the rich snake of a man who had swindled her.

From the jaws of defeat, victory.

She smiled as she unrolled her sleeping bag and thought again of Adam. What had happened when he'd knocked on Harlan Rockwood's front door. What had he *done?*

Would he tell Beth?

No. No, Char didn't have to worry about that. Adam would never upset his sister by telling her that her best friend might very well be mixed up with her ex-husband.

Might very well be indeed. But she wasn't going to ruin her mood by thinking about Harlan . . . or about Adam. Was he cursing her from thirty thousand feet up?

"Thank you, Adam," she said to herself, "but I'm so glad you're back in Vermont."

And she crawled into her sleeping bag, amazed at how good life looked when she knew she wouldn't have to face slugs in her shoes in the morning.

ADAM ARRIVED back in Vermont at midnight, turned up at the sawmill at eight the next morning and had his sister to dinner that evening. He refused to discuss Charity Bradford until David and Abby went out to the den to work their latest thousand-piece jigsaw puzzle. The evening air was cool enough to build fires in the two wood stoves, one of the first tasks Adam had learned to manage one-handed. He had never even considered giving up his life-style in the hills above Millbrook; he and Julian and Beth had built his post-and-beam house overlooking the rushing, clear, rocky Mill Brook. Six months after he, Mel and the kids had moved in, his wife finally admitted she hated living so far out of town. Why had she pretended enthusiasm for the project when she had felt none? *For your sake, Adam*, she had told him. *I couldn't bear to disappoint you.* Even now his insides burned with guilt at the memory of her words.

Never again would he permit anyone to do anything for his sake. He could live with disappointment and compromise better than he could guilt. And he had learned to demand honesty and openness from the people around him—most of all, from himself. Mel and he had drifted apart. If she had refused to see what had happened between them, he should have. Perhaps they could have worked out the problems in their marriage; perhaps not. But a resolution, in favor or against staying together, would have been preferable to the state of siege that had existed between them in the last months of Mel's life.

Now she was dead. His children had lost their mother, and Adam had lost his naivety. He no longer readily believed what people said. It didn't follow that just because he never said what he didn't mean everyone else did the same. Now he always asked himself what was percolating underneath other people's words. What were the hidden agendas? What weren't they telling him, for his sake or their own?

What, for example, hadn't Char told him?

And what wasn't his sister telling him?

He brought her a mug of hot mulled cider and sat cross-legged with her on the thick carpet in front of the living room wood stove. Solid, dependable, no-nonsense Beth. She could operate any saw at the mill, do any job, take over for either of her brothers, as they could for her. She drove the shabbiest car in Millbrook and rented a saltbox house in the village, built shortly after the end of the War of 1812 with wood cut on Mill Brook Post & Beam's old water-powered up-and-down saw. The place was starting to crumble, but she, ever the optimist, believed it could be saved with a little sweat and Yankee ingenuity. She preferred, she claimed, to live a simple life.

It hadn't always been that way. Tawny-haired, green-eyed and more attractive than she liked to admit, Beth had shared her best friend Char's childhood dream of getting out of Millbrook. At eighteen, when she chose Vanderbilt University in Nashville over the New England colleges that had accepted her, Beth had made her own bid for independence. She met wealthy, charming Harlan Rockwood as an undergraduate; he was a second-year law student. They had married six months later, against the powerful Rockwood family's wishes. They stayed in Nashville.

In the shadow of the Rockwoods their marriage began to flounder within a year, but Beth wasn't a quitter. Trying to ignore her unhappiness, she threw herself into one upwardly mobile job after another until her whole life came apart at the seams. She left her husband, left her high-profile sales jobs, left the posh life being a Rockwood had afforded her. She came home to Millbrook and the Stiles family business, and if she hadn't had much to do with men since Harlan, it was her doing.

More than one man from Vermont had approached Adam for background information on his sister, which he refused to provide. If they wanted to know about Elizabeth Stiles, they would have to find out for themselves. Many tried. But although she enjoyed an occasional evening out, Beth wasn't looking for a permanent relationship. Men, she liked to insist, were babies—her brothers excluded, of course: She preferred to put her time and energy into logs.

Beth sipped her hot cider while Adam related his frustrating trip to Tennessee. Even while he talked he had to repress images of Char and Emily in the sticky heat of their tent on the Cumberland River. They didn't have to live that way. If Char knew so damn much about everything, why didn't she know that?

"Char's stubborn," Beth said finally, explaining the obvious. "And she's proud."

Adam scowled. "She's cutting off her nose to spite her face."

"Maybe. I'm not sure we have the right to judge without all the facts."

"All what facts?"

Beth lifted her shoulders in a half-innocent shrug, but didn't meet her older brother's eye. "Well, we don't have Char's side of the story. There might be a logical explanation for everything she's done. Adam, you know you rub her the wrong way. She might have been pulling your string the whole time."

"Charity Bradford isn't a game player," Adam pointed out. "You know that. Beth, what aren't you telling me?"

"Nothing . . ."

"You never could lie worth a damn. You know something about this business that you don't want me to know. So far you've done all the listening and I've done all the talking."

Beth gave him an irritated look. "I haven't seen Char since she left Millbrook. How would I know what she's up to?"

"You've been friends forever."

"So? Adam, I'm not defending her. I'm just trying to be objective—"

"Are you denying you were worried about her?"

"No!"

"Then why are you squirming?"

"I am not squirming. Look, I'm not going to sit here and be interrogated by my own brother!"

She had a point. But after the way Char had treated him—after the way he had reacted to her and *still* couldn't get the soft shape of her mouth out of his mind—Adam had to admit to a certain lack of objectivity, not to mention patience. He couldn't blame Beth for holding back on him. He was doing the same to her. He had told her everything about his trip to Tennessee, except for one telling, crucial fact; that Char was mixed up somehow with Beth's ex-husband. From Beth's tepid reaction to the goings-on in Nashville, Adam had to assume she didn't know about Harlan Rockwood's apparent involvement in Char's problems.

So what *did* his sister know that she wasn't telling him?

He drank some of his own cider, suddenly wishing, in a jumble of emotions he couldn't seem to sort out, that Char were there with him.

Good Lord, what was happening to him?

He was a sane, practical, stable man. He didn't lust after crazy women who lived in tents. He didn't lie awake nights thinking about them. After his confrontation with Ginger, Harlan Rockwood's housekeeper, he had raced back to Char's campsite and found little more than pounded grass and fish bones to indicate she had even been there. She had pulled up stakes and fled while he was off on another wild-goose chase. Whatever she was, Charity Bradford was no dummy. If she had been on the river when he had returned from the latest Southern mansion she didn't live in, there was no telling what he would have done. The idea made him uncomfortable; he didn't like not being able to predict his own actions.

Or maybe he was just pretending he didn't know exactly what he would have done. Throughout his flight to Boston, his ride back to Vermont and his long, lonely night at home, he had imagined not strangling Char for her shenanigans, but making love to her in that damn sweaty tent of hers.

He had hoped being back in his own time zone and on New England's rocky soil would help knock some sense back into him.

So far, not so good.

"Char has her own way of doing things," Beth said, cutting into her brother's wandering thoughts. Another bad sign: he wasn't the kind of man whose mind wandered.

"What things?"

"Maybe land prices were higher than she anticipated and she's living in a tent so she can save every nickel to buy her spread. You know Char. She doesn't do anything halfway."

"Beth, she's living in a tent because she's broke."

"You don't know that," Beth snapped.

"There, you see?" Adam countered. "You are defending her."

"I'm not. You don't like her, so you're hot to hang her from the nearest tree."

"My mind has run more toward drowning."

"There, you see? You have her tried and convicted!"

"Damn right." He settled back against the bottom of the couch, stretching out his legs, perfectly aware he was goading his sister. "What more evidence do I need?"

"Maybe there were..." Beth bit her lip, then plunged in and finished, "mitigating circumstances."

Now he was getting somewhere. "Such as?"

"You shouldn't complain about Char," Beth grumbled. "You'd have made a hell of a lawyer yourself. Most people you could cut in two with those eyes of yours. You can be such a bastard, Adam. Damn it, quit looking at me like that!"

"What are you hiding?"

"Adam—"

"Tell me, Beth, or I'm on the phone to Char's ex-husband telling him he ought to sue for custody of his daughter because her mother's got her living in a tent."

Beth grew very still. "You wouldn't."

"In fifteen seconds I will."

"Adam, this is none of your business."

"You made it my business when you asked me to check on Char. I'm counting."

Beth groaned. "And Char used to wish *she* had older brothers."

"Eight seconds."

"It would kill her to lose Emily. It would kill Emily."

"She'd have a proper bed. She could take a bath, for God's sake." Adam climbed to his feet. "Time's up."

Beth remained on the floor, but said something in a small voice.

Adam spun around, thinking he'd heard right but not believing—praying—he hadn't. "Say that again," he ordered.

Scowling, Beth repeated what Adam thought he'd heard. "Char invested almost all of her money in a horse."

"*A* horse?"

All Beth could do was nod.

"Millicent left her at least forty grand, and she had her savings and her profits from selling her house. Are you telling me she bet it all on a damn horse?"

"Not bet. Invested."

"There are no guarantees with horses. You don't bet money you can't afford to lose."

Beth stiffened. "Char knew the risks." Then, slumping all at once, she added, "So did I."

"You?"

"Since you know everything else, you might as well know that I had Char invest twenty thousand for me."

Adam clenched his hand at his side and kept himself from shouting. "You can't afford to lose twenty thousand."

"I know, but . . ." She refused to finish.

"But what?"

Beth climbed to her feet and grabbed her coat off the couch. "It doesn't matter."

"Beth, please." Adam touched her arm with a gentleness that amazed him. But he had seen the pain—the worry—in her eyes. "Tell me."

"Char guaranteed my investment."

"She *what?*"

"There's no financial risk for me. She insisted."

Adam's short-lived calm vanished, and he felt as if he would explode. His hand dropped from his sister's side as he backed off and looked for something to throw, something to relieve the pent-up frustration he was feeling, the sheer impotence.

He swung back around at Beth. "Right now your buddy Char can't even guarantee herself a hot meal, never mind your twenty grand!"

"Adam . . ." Now all at once Beth looked scared; he could see her swallow. "Do you think something happened to the horse?"

"You mean you've got twenty thousand dollars invested with her and you don't know what's going on?"

"No. Char keeps assuring me everything's fine, but—"

"But she also told you she lives in a museum."

"I'm worried," Beth said simply.

Adam exhaled. "I know."

"Not about me—about Char. You know how she is."

Yes, he did. Charity Winnifred Bradford was the last person he knew who would ever admit to failure. Adam was suddenly glad his instincts had kept him from bringing up Harlan Rockwood's name. There was no point in adding to his sister's concerns, at least not until he had more information. Had Char dragged Harlan into her scheme as well? Impossible. Not even she was that crazy.

"I wish I knew what to do," Beth said.

"You don't do anything," Adam advised without hesitation. "You're too close to Char and you've got too much riding on whatever the hell it is she's up to. Let me see what I can do."

Beth's green eyes widened suddenly, and she gave her brother a surprised, knowing look that suggested she had a fair idea of what had been going on in his mind since he had watched Char walk across the beautiful grounds of Belle Meade to her car two days ago.

"Thanks, Adam," his sister said judiciously.

He grunted. "No thanks needed. Your buddy gave me the runaround one time too many. I'm not going to make any promises, but I'll do what I can to find out what's really going on with that lunatic."

5

THE WEEKENDS WHEN EMILY flew to New York to be with her father were the most difficult for Char, but at least they came only once a month. She had hoped she would cope better in their new cottage than the tent, but the emptiness of the tiny house, Em's drawings on the refrigerator, her bath toys in the basket next to the tub, only served to remind Char of her aloneness. In Vermont she had never really minded Emily's monthly visits with her father. She would use the time to catch up on work, go to movies and concerts without having to pay a baby-sitter, just be alone with a fire in the fireplace and a good book to read. Tennessee wasn't like that for her, not yet. If she had more furniture, she supposed she might feel more at ease. But maybe not. There was more to her restlessness than not owning a sofa; it had to do with lost dreams and failure and a deep, swelling, endless fury with herself for ever having been dumb enough to get swindled out of everything she had.

Harlan Rockwood had betrayed her trust. She would prove it and make him answer for what he had done.

The thought of retribution got her out of bed and off to work on the quiet, delightfully cool Saturday morning without Emily, just over a week after Adam Stiles had intruded into their lives and launched Char into a house she couldn't afford.

Today was her last day at Belle Meade. Monday she began work at a cosmetics counter at a moderate-priced department store in downtown Nashville. She had given up on the legal profession until she had her credentials together to practice law in the state of Tennessee. In the meantime her boss at the department store had subtly let her wishes be known on the subject of Char's fingernails, namely that she ought to grow them. Char supposed painting her nails magenta wasn't nearly as bad a fate as typing letters for a sleazy lawyer. Not that she wouldn't have taken that job if offered.

Such was the state of her desperation.

At least Emily liked the idea of magenta fingernail polish.

Char's last day at Belle Meade flew by, and maybe because she had only her empty house and an immediate future behind a cosmetics counter to look forward to, she thought about Adam far more than she would have liked . . . or ever have admitted. All week she had expected to walk out to her car and find him sitting on the hood, ready to strangle her. There hadn't been a word from him since she had sent him off to Harlan Rockwood's. Nor had she heard from Beth. If Adam had realized Char was squatting on Rockwood land and had told Beth, there would have been no keeping her in Vermont. So either Adam hadn't realized it or hadn't told Beth.

Char hated not knowing for sure, but finding out entailed at least a phone call to Vermont. Best to leave well enough alone on that score.

Most likely Adam had figured she had made it clear she wanted him to mind his own business, decided to respect her wishes and gone back to his logs. She had no idea why that prospect depressed her, but it did. Was she so damn desperate to have someone care about her that even Adam, who didn't even like her, would do?

Suddenly she missed her Great-Aunt Millicent so much she could have cried. Aunt Mil had cared about her. She had been the one person in the world whose unconditional love Char had known she could count on. She could have told Aunt Mil everything.

She said goodbye to her friends at Belle Meade and started out to her car, the loneliness of that morning returning in full force. In spite of her wish not to, she remembered Adam's smile and his laugh and his generosity with Emily at dinner. If she didn't settle up with Harlan Rockwood and get on with her life soon, she just might end up doing something crazier than investing her life savings, her inheritance and her best friend's money in a crummy horse.

The only thing crazier than *that* would be renewing her twelve-year-old's crush on Adam Stiles.

That wouldn't be crazy. That would be downright laughable.

And just as futile as expecting her beautiful, expensive Thoroughbred would win a race against anyone except kids on bicycles.

With her job at Belle Meade finished, she suddenly realized, anyone coming down to Tennessee would have a tough time locating her. She tried to tell herself it was just as well; she didn't need anyone meddling in her affairs right now. But as she approached her car, she had to acknowledge the gnawing of panic in her gut . . . in her very soul. She was on her own.

Then she stopped dead and decided she was seeing things. Too much desperation, too much loneliness, too much introspection. Too much caffeine. Something.

She blinked once, twice, three times and all she got for her effort was dizzy.

Adam Stiles remained on the hood of her car.

He looked every inch the uncompromising Yankee he was, but Char couldn't hold back a giddy smile—until she remembered she had given the man cause to be very angry with her indeed. Then she stopped smiling and told herself to be sensible. She had dug herself a large hole with this man. Best to consider ways to climb out of it without his wanting to boot her back in.

"Adam? That *is* you."

She laughed the kind of laugh lawyers made when clients popped into the office unannounced. It sounded forced, which it was. Not only did she have simple shock to contend with, not to mention her loneliness without Emily, her apprehension about starting her new job and her feelings of disorientation at moving to a new house. But she also had to deal with something more elemental, something primitive and unexpected and utterly impossible to deny. And that was her simple, raw awareness of the man. Of *Adam*. It was like suddenly finding the neighbor's German shepherd, whom you had considered mean and unapproachable for years, as dopey and friendly as a golden retriever puppy.

Bad analogy, Char thought. She wasn't all at once finding Adam dopey and friendly. Sexy and desirable were more like it.

He wasn't wearing his hook, but that wasn't what she noticed first. His eyes were. They were dark and narrowed and not very pleased.

"Good gracious," she went on, falling on her favorite old Southern expression. "What a surprise. Are you back in Nashville on business?"

"You could say that."

His voice was deep and serious, his words clipped in that Yankee way. Char had gotten so accustomed to the pleasant rhythms of the South that she was even more attuned to every nuance of his voice, taking nothing for granted. There was no drawl to mitigate the knee-wobbling effect of his words . . . just his eyes. Focused on her as intently as they were, they brimmed not with controlled anger or even cool neutrality, but with the same confusion Char herself was feeling. Or maybe she was projecting her own emotions onto him, deciding he felt what she wanted him to feel—what she herself felt.

In fact, she wouldn't be surprised if he had deliberately sought her out, because Adam Stiles wasn't a man to let anyone have the last word.

"Oh?" She couldn't think of much else to say that wouldn't sound defensive or antagonistic or plain dumb. "Tell me more."

"In the car."

"Mine? Where's yours?"

"I took a cab from the airport."

Must have cost a pretty penny. "Directly here?"

Almost a smile. "You got it."

Not good, Char thought. Not good at all. It wouldn't be easy to get rid of him this time. "Adam, if you came all the way to Tennessee just for revenge because I jerked you around a little—"

"Not a little, Char. A lot."

"You had it coming to you."

"How so?"

She didn't know how so, except that he had stopped in to see a friend while he was in town and unknowingly had pulled the rug out from under the life she had fashioned for herself for the folks back home in Vermont. But she had to say something. "You shouldn't have been so relentless."

His eyes grew warm as they searched hers. "I thought I was just being a friend."

"You should have guessed." She cleared her throat, hating his sincerity. His gentleness. Why couldn't he be mad? "Never mind. What's your revenge to be?"

He didn't rise to her bait, but simply shook his head. "I don't want revenge."

"Then what do you want?"

"Answers, I guess."

She laughed bitterly. "Don't we all."

IF SHE WASN'T GOING to give Adam answers, Char decided she should stop telling him lies. At least not so many. She drove Adam to her little rented house outside Nashville and sat him at what passed for a kitchen table: a white-painted board over two sawhorses. What furniture she hadn't sold was in storage in Vermont. Emily had picked a bunch of black-eyed Susans, which Char had put in a jelly jar and sat in the middle of her makeshift table, and they had found a couple of folding wooden chairs that sort of matched. Add a couple of sky-blue place mats and Char found she didn't particularly miss her antique Shaker table in storage in Vermont.

Adam sat on one of the folding chairs while Char put on the kettle for coffee. The ease with which she could now boil water continued to delight her. *Ah, to appreciate the little things in life.* From what she had observed of Adam over the years, she supposed he already did.

One point in his favor, anyway.

He looked around the simple kitchen. "This isn't Belle Meade or Cheekwood," he observed, "and it sure as hell isn't the Rockwood estate, but it does have your stamp on it. And it's better than that tent of yours."

Char shrugged as she got her coffeepot and filter and two mugs down from the open shelves. "I don't know. A couple of nights Emily and I have missed our tent. Reading aloud under a proper roof just isn't the same."

"How long were you on the river?"

"Just a month."

Adam sat very still, his eyes narrowed, capable, it seemed, of peering into her very soul. "Why?"

"We'd rented a farmhouse," Char explained, squelching the urge to lie. "Nothing fancy, but nice. There was a big porch with a swing, and blackberry bushes and a gorgeous view of the river. The rent was fair, but not cheap." With a sigh she spooned coffee into the filter. She used to buy gourmet beans and grind them herself; now she settled for whatever was on sale at the grocery store. "I kept us there as long as I could."

"It was furnished?"

Char nodded. "What furniture I didn't sell when we left Vermont I had stored. I saved a few of Mother's and Aunt Millicent's pieces—antiques, that sort of thing. I figured I'd have everything shipped when we got settled. I didn't want to rent a trailer and drag a lot of stuff down."

"Understandably," Adam said in a tone that told Char he hadn't understood anything she had done.

She leaned against the counter as the kettle began to hiss and quickly took in this hard, quiet man, wondering what about her had prompted him to leave Vermont and the mill for a second time in a week. Not his style. She said, "I'm not trying to justify my actions to you."

"Why didn't you call someone from home for help?"

"Who? Beth? My clients? *You?*"

"I'd have helped," he said simply, without drama.

Yes, he would have. So would Beth and his brother Julian. So would dozens of others from Millbrook and the surrounding towns. So would her ex-husband, if it had come to that.

"I can handle my own problems," she said tightly.

"I know how you feel." His voice was surprisingly quiet, nonjudgmental, even gentle. "I've learned the hard way that to ask for help isn't always a sign of weakness, but often a measure of strength. You're independent and hardheaded, Char. Always have been. Doesn't mean you need to go it alone all the time."

Ignoring him, Char swung around and grabbed the kettle before it had a chance to whistle, dampening the grounds with the near-boiling water. She waited impatiently for the water to soak in, her grip on the kettle tight. To her relief Adam kept quiet. She could feel his gaze on her and feigned composure, knowing he couldn't see her knuckles whitening on the kettle handle.

You're just making coffee for an old family friend, she told herself while she went ahead and admitted she had wrecked her life and didn't have a single person she felt comfortable turning to for help or even solace. Aunt Mil was dead. Her father had died when Char was fourteen, and her mother had disengaged herself from her daughter years ago and lived in Florida. Except for Em, Char thought, she was pretty much alone in the world and might as well admit it.

"Are you going to tell me what happened?" Adam asked softly.

"What'll you do if I don't?" Her tone was belligerent, and she banged the kettle back down onto the stove.

Adam didn't respond. The only sound in the kitchen was the drip of the coffee into the glass carafe. When it finished, she filled the two mugs and set them on the table. She remembered Adam didn't take milk or sugar, one of those useless tidbits that cluttered her brain. It came from a morning not long after his accident when she, as his lawyer, had come to his house to discuss his legal affairs. Still in considerable pain, he had insisted on making her coffee. He wasn't yet used to working one-handed, but she had had the good grace, for a change, to keep her mouth shut and let him get the job done in his own good time. Without her help. Eventually he'd learned to manage most anything one-handed or with the use of his hook. Beth said he could even tie his work boots using just his right hand.

Maybe, Char thought, that experience, that need to adapt to his disability on his own, would help him see that he had to butt out of her business now.

Then again, maybe not. This was Adam, and she wasn't missing a hand.

"If I have to," he said finally, his tone heating up, "I'll knock on Harlan Rockwood's door and ask him what he knows about the mess you're in."

Just what she needed. Harlan and Adam—a couple of know-it-all men, one of them a crook—discussing her over a fifth of bourbon. Beth *had* warned Char to steer clear of her ex-husband. "Tennessee's a beautiful state and there are a ton of nice people there," Beth had told her, "but do not—do *not*—go near Harlan Rockwood. He'll use you to get back at me."

And indeed he had.

For the moment.

Char restrained herself and managed to give Adam a cool look. "Harlan will say he doesn't know anything about me or the mess I'm in."

"Will he be lying?"

"Adam, let's just have a cup of coffee together and forget about everything else." She held her mug in her hands, welcoming its warmth against her suddenly icy fingers. "How're Abby and David doing?"

"Fine. Beth took them hiking this weekend. Nothing like walking in the New England woods this time of year, in my opinion." His eyes rested on her just a split-second longer than necessary. "Join us sometime?"

"Sure. I'll just pop on up. It's only—what, a thousand miles?" But she could see her sarcasm wasn't going over well with Adam, knew it wasn't going over well with herself. Her stomach hurt, and she could recall the sweet, unique smells of ripe apples being pressed into the famous Stiles cider. She sniffed her coffee, just to get that nostalgic scent from her memory. "Have the leaves turned?"

"The reds and bright oranges are all out, most of the yellows. We should be at peak next weekend. Char—" Adam bit off her name, as if saying it made *his* stomach hurt. He sighed. "Char, if I have to I'll beat the truth out of Harlan. He's no friend of mine."

"I am?"

"You have to ask? You're Beth's friend. That makes you important to me."

Beth's friend. Was that all she was to him? *Lordy! What more do you expect? What more do you want? This is Adam we're talking about!*

She cleared her throat, wondering if inexpensive coffee destroyed rational thinking. "You don't want to see Beth hurt."

Adam looked at her. "Or you."

She laughed, in spite of herself. "Too late for that! As for Beth..." Char sighed, wishing she could press some kind of internal rewind button and start all over again. She had already told Adam too damn much for her own good. "Did you tell her I'd sent you to Rockwood's house?"

"What do you think?"

"Probably not. If you had, there's no telling what Beth would have done, but I doubt she'd be taking Abby and David hiking."

Adam nodded. "She'd be down here wringing Harlan's neck. He sold you your horse?"

Char quickly drank a mouthful of coffee to hide her surprise at Adam's question. How much did he know already? Was *he* playing games with *her*? If she wasn't known as a game player, Adam—well, Adam Stiles took the prize when it came to straight-up, no-nonsense Yankee curmudgeons.

She said, "You've been prying information out of Beth, haven't you?"

"It wasn't easy," Adam said without apology. "She's loyal to you, Char, but she's also worried. Rightly so, in my opinion."

Char set down her mug, not as hard as she felt like. "I'm a big girl—"

"You're out on a limb in a hurricane and you're so damn stiff-necked you'd rather ride out the storm than let someone give you a hand down."

His face had gotten red and his voice had risen, although he wasn't shouting. Adam, she recalled, seldom shouted. He didn't need to. People usually backed down just with one of his famous looks. The man was intimidating.

Char wasn't intimidated.

"What would you do in my place?" she asked calmly.

Adam grunted, clearly annoyed. "I don't know what 'your place' is. Tell me and I'll tell you what I'd do. Char," he went on, rising from his chair, "all I'm offering is my friendship."

"You're not offering friendship, Adam. You're shoving it down my throat."

He said nothing, just marched over to the counter and poured himself another cup of coffee.

"Okay," Char said, equivocating.

Adam turned around and leaned against the counter, looking ever the woodsman. She noticed the length of his legs, the tough, bulging muscles of his thighs and chest. Married to Mel and then a guilt-ridden widower, he had been off-limits to Char for years, and she had simply not considered him in any sexual way. Now she couldn't imagine how she had resisted. Every fiber of the man exuded masculinity.

She sprang to her feet. "Look, I need a little time to think. If you were Beth...hell, Adam, if you were anybody but you I'd know whether to confide in you or send you packing. But we've got a history, you know. I mean— Adam, to be honest, I'd never considered you a friend."

He surprised her with a grin, raking his eyes over her. "Sweetheart, the feeling's mutual."

Her mouth snapped shut. "I didn't mean you *weren't* a friend."

He laughed. "I know what you meant. Will you have dinner with me tonight?"

"Of course. I'll meet you at your hotel—"

"No hotel."

She grew very still, just waiting.

"I'm staying here." He moved closer to her, invading her space . . . shattering her elusive sense of stability. "Even brought my own sleeping bag. I saw Em's. Dinosaurs don't suit me."

Right then, Char wasn't so sure about that.

ADAM TOOK ONE LOOK in Char's refrigerator and decided they had better have dinner out or hit the nearest grocery. Even in her solvent days she had never been much on stocking up. She had lived within walking distance of the Millbrook Country Store and fetched what she needed when she needed it or just made do.

"You're into legumes these days," he commented, examining the equally meager contents of her cupboards.

"They're good for you."

"Emily likes them?"

"She eats them. She'd live on boxed macaroni and cheese and canned string beans if I let her."

Adam didn't mention he could go for a little boxed macaroni and cheese over the stuff lurking in Char's old natural peanut butter and no-sugar jam jars.

"I could whip up some spicy kasha," she offered.

"Thanks, no."

She was sitting at her makeshift kitchen table, calm now that he had stopped pressing her for truth and honesty. "The key with grains and legumes," she said, "is the right herbs and spices."

"Or thinking like a horse," Adam muttered.

Char frowned at the mention of horses: not a good subject. "I've got some catfish in the freezer. I could broil up a few with salsa and . . . I don't know, white beans."

"Let's hit the grocery. We've got tomorrow to think about, as well. Don't you ever get the urge for good Vermont cheese?"

"I eat cheese in moderation," she said loftily. "Have to watch the fat content. Now Vermont maple syrup— that I miss. I can get it here in certain places, but it's so expensive. To think we used to get sick on it every March when we were kids. Look, if we're going to the grocery, I've got to stop and get some cash."

"My treat."

Her expression grew dark, remote. "Dinner last weekend was your treat."

"And this weekend I'm an uninvited guest." Adam shut the cupboard door, aware he was on thin ice again. "If I hadn't shown up, what would you eat for supper?"

"Curried lentils, probably. They're not Em's favorite, so I save them for when she's away. They're delicious—and good for you."

"I'm sure. Another day, Char."

She gave up on trying to talk him into lentils, kasha, bulgur or—and here Adam really drew the line—dried fermented bean curd. Instead she drove him to a monstrous grocery store, where she pushed the cart while he pulled items off the shelves.

"Just enough for the weekend," Char warned. "I'm not a charity case."

Adam glowered at her. "Maybe you should be. Or would you rather starve?"

She sniffed, an improvement over a couple of hours ago when she probably would have blown her stack. "I'd go back to Vermont before I'd let Emily starve."

"If it were just you?"

"That's a speculative question. It's not just me."

"Lawyer talk." He ignore her dark looks and pulled anything he felt like from the shelves: crackers, cereal, oatmeal, chocolate chips, flour, a few packages of macaroni and cheese for Em's sake. When he saw Char ready to blow a gasket, he just smiled at her and said, "I don't know what I might be in the mood to eat tomorrow— I want to be prepared."

"What are the chocolate chips for?"

"Just in case I feel like making cookies."

"You can't. I don't have vanilla or baking soda."

So he tossed the biggest jar of vanilla and the biggest box of baking soda he could find into the cart. Char just glared at him. In her glory days as a New York lawyer, and even as a Vermont lawyer, she could have fed half of Millbrook on her earnings.

Life as a gentlewoman horse farmer apparently hadn't met her expectations.

Why, Adam wondered, did that thought not particularly bother him?

Because Charity Bradford was a survivor, yes. Because she was a lawyer, not a horsewoman. Yes, that, too. Because she belonged in Vermont. Damn right, he believed that. Because she had no business in Nashville, Tennessee. True.

But there was more to his perverse neutrality, if not out-and-out satisfaction, toward her apparent failure at raising horses. He wanted Char to be happy, he realized. And he didn't believe she would be happy chasing some damn childhood dream that hadn't made sense when she was ten and sure as hell didn't make sense now.

It wasn't even that, however. Char had to make up her own mind about what made her happy and what didn't. No, Adam thought, as much as he wanted Char to be happy, he wasn't thinking about her when he reacted to her misfortunes. He was thinking about himself.

He wanted her back in Vermont.

Ignoring the exorbitant price and Char's grimace, he tossed a quart of pure Vermont maple syrup into the cart.

"Pancakes and sausages for breakfast?" he suggested.

"I don't have any sausages."

"You do have a frying pan?"

She gave him one of her prickly looks, telling him better than words could that he was pushing it.

The sausage department was bigger than any he had ever seen in Vermont. Char recommended a spicy local brand, apparently her legume kick not deterring her from anything as high-fat, high-salt and plain *good* as sausage.

Here he had come to wring the truth out of her and instead he was making up possible menus for Sunday breakfast ... which was preferable, he supposed, to thinking about how they were going to get through the night in that tiny house. On the flight from Nashville he had carefully worked out the logistics of spending the night in her tent: he wouldn't. Not that he had intended to give Char the chance to abscond again by staying in a hotel. He would just lay in his sleeping bag on the ground in front of her tent and camp out under the stars.

He had counted on that tent.

He had counted, too, on Emily being around.

Now here they were, Char and himself, shopping for groceries and planning to spend the night in a cozy cottage like a pair of honeymooners. Madness.

His only consolation was that he hadn't been invited and Char would likely boot him out if she had the chance.

If only, he thought, she didn't look so stubborn and confident and forlorn and more damn beautiful than he ever remembered, even the day she had married that uptight New York lawyer. Had she changed that much in the past year? Or had he just never really bothered to see her before?

The grocery tab came to just over a hundred dollars.

"Quite a weekend you're planning," Char grumbled.

"Us Vermont mountain men have big appetites."

"You'd better. We've got enough food here for a month."

"That's an exaggeration, Char, even the way you've been eating. Course, I might decide to stay a month unless you start talking."

She didn't answer him, just stalked off ahead of him, leaving Adam to push the cart to her beat-up car. "It's tough," he said as she opened the rusting hatchback without a word, "when your vision of yourself doesn't fit the reality."

"You don't know anything about my vision of myself."

He shrugged, hefting a bag of groceries. "You wouldn't want to be mistress of Belle Meade?"

"It's a museum," she snapped.

"Now that sounds more like Millbrook's own feet-flat-on-the-floor Charity Winnifred. What about mistress of the Rockwood estate?"

Char scoffed, grabbing a bag of groceries. "The only involvement I want with the Rockwood estate is setting it on fire."

"Aha. So Harlan did have something to do with your downfall."

But Char was staring into the bag of groceries she'd lowered into the back of her car. "Adam— Adam, what's this?"

He had a peek. "Country ham."

"That stuff'll harden your arteries just from reading the ingredients label!"

"Bet it's good, though."

She made a face. "I guess we could soak some of the salt out . . ."

That was close enough to victory for him. He got the last of the groceries into the car while Char darted into the front seat, thinking, no doubt, her comment about the ham had diverted him from the subject of Harlan Rockwood.

He hoped she knew him better than that.

He climbed in beside her. "The horse you and Beth invested in came from Harlan, didn't it? The investment went sour, you lost your shirt and you don't want to tell Beth her ex-husband has her twenty grand."

Char's knuckles were turning white from her grip on the steering wheel.

"Have I hit the nail on the head?" Adam asked casually.

"Except for one thing.'

Char spoke quietly, but her voice was tight and her grip hadn't slackened on the poor wheel. Adam, however, couldn't bring himself to feel sorry for her. Pity would just have made her madder, and since she had gotten herself into this predicament and could easily get herself out by returning to Millbrook and dusting off her lawyer's shingle and renewing her many friend-ships, he didn't figure he owed her an overabundance of sympathy. He would save that for victims of earth-quakes and famine.

But he *was* curious . . . and concerned. Char seemed to be in a state in which she couldn't see the forest for the trees. When she didn't go on, he said, "What one thing?"

"My deal with Harlan wasn't on the up-and-up."

"What do you mean?"

"I mean," she said with difficulty, "he swindled me."

"And by extension, Beth?"

"Yes."

Adam couldn't help himself: he had to laugh. He was incredulous. Amazed. "I'm sorry," he said, "but the idea of anyone swindling Charity Bradford and getting away with it—"

"He won't get away with it forever."

Adam stopped laughing and chose his next words more carefully. "Maybe not. But, Char, what in God's name else would you expect Harlan Rockwood to do to his ex-wife's best friend? The poor bastard probably couldn't help himself."

Too late, he realized he had said the wrong thing. She slammed on the brakes and pulled over to the side of the road. "Out," she commanded.

"Char—"

She wouldn't look at him. "Get out of my car, Adam. I won't have you judging me."

"I wasn't judging you."

"No? Would *you* have bought a horse from Harlan Rockwood?"

"Speculative."

"You as much as called me a fool."

Adam sighed. "You're not a fool."

"Only a fool would go into a deal with Harlan."

"You misunderstood me," he said in a neutral tone, but his own blood was beginning to boil. Why the hell was he on the hot seat?

She glare at him. "Oh?"

"We can discuss this back at the house."

"Put it in a letter," she said nastily. "Go call a cab, Adam. You're spending the night in a hotel."

He just looked at her. Her cheeks were flushed, she was breathing hard, her hands still had their death grip on the steering wheel. The woman was fighting mad. He figured it was a good sign: she hadn't given herself up to defeat.

Finally he asked, "What about all our food?"

"I'll take it back to the grocery and send you a check."

"I was counting on Tennessee sausage for breakfast."

"Ask at your hotel," she said, stubborn as ever.

"Char, I'm not getting out of this car."

"I'll kick you out."

He leaned in closer to her; he could see the drops of perspiration on her upper lip. "Try."

Her breath caught. He could hear it. She looked at him, their eyes barely twelve inches apart, her mouth slightly open. He watched her tongue slide over her lower lip, dampening it, and for a moment he thought he could taste the salty sweetness of her mouth on his.

Maybe a hotel wasn't such a bad idea.

"We both need to cool off," he said.

"Yeah." She cleared her throat and popped the car back into gear, tearing her eyes from him as she checked her side mirror for traffic. "I guess we do."

In more ways than one, Adam thought, determined to keep his mouth shut for the rest of the trip back to her house.

6

THEIR TRUCE LASTED long enough to get the groceries into the kitchen. Char still smarted over Adam's obvious belief that *he* never would have bought a share in any horse owned by Harlan Rockwood, as if he knew anything about men and horses. He did know Harlan, however, and pointed that out in no uncertain terms when Char continued to grumble.

"Beth may be finished with Harlan," Adam said as he loaded up the kitchen shelves with boxes, bags, jars and cans, "but he's not finished with her."

Char scoffed. "He is, too. They've been divorced for years. They haven't even seen each other since I don't know when."

"Has Harlan remarried?"

"No—"

"Has Beth remarried?"

"You know she hasn't."

With his precious pound of sausage tucked under his left arm, he opened up the refrigerator. "I rest my case."

Char went after six cans of tomato paste in the bottom of a bag. *Six* cans. They'd never use that much in one weekend. Where was her pride? She lined them up on a shelf, almost giddy at the sight of so much food in one place.

"What *is* your case?" she asked irritably.

Adam said with equanimity, "You should never have gone into business with Harlan Rockwood."

"No kidding."

"I'm not trying to criticize you," he said, carefully lifting the Vermont maple syrup from a bag, "and I doubt I'd have done any better raising horses than you have."

"But if I'd asked, you'd have told me to steer clear of Beth's ex-husband."

He set the maple syrup on the shelf next to her cans of tomato paste. "Yes."

"I didn't ask. And, anyway, your reasoning's all wrong on why I should have avoided Harlan. He doesn't even know Beth's my partner."

"He knows Beth's your best friend."

"So?"

"So it'd be a logical assumption on his part that he could get to her through you."

"But he hasn't."

Adam turned around and leaned against the counter. "Who has Beth's twenty grand?"

"I do."

"You mean you didn't invest her money?"

"No, I did."

"Then Harlan has it."

"Technically, yes. But I can repay Beth."

"With your own money?"

Char nodded, already wishing she had beaten Adam Stiles out of her car and retreated when she'd had the chance. This conversation wasn't getting her anywhere she wanted to go.

"You mean," Adam said in a deadly tone, "that you have twenty thousand dollars in the bank? And you've been living in a damn *tent*? You've been eating beans and sleeping in a sleeping bag?" He groaned. "Char, have you lost your mind?"

"I guaranteed Beth's money," she said simply.

Adam swore.

"Look, my financial affairs aren't your concern. And I doubt Harlan Rockwood swindled me because he wanted to get back at Beth or get back into her life or whatever. He swindled me because he's a sleazeball and dishonesty comes naturally to him."

"You've been listening to Beth," Adam remarked, snatching up an empty paper bag and folding it. With his deft movements, no one would even notice he was missing a hand. "Harlan's never struck me as dishonest. He and Beth were too young when they got married, and Beth made a mistake when she thought she had to out-Rockwood the Rockwoods. But I can't say that makes him a sleazeball."

"Swindling me does."

"Did you approach him about a deal or did he approach you?"

"Seeing how I was a Vermont lawyer up until last year and never owned a horse in my life, what do you think?"

Adam smiled, amused. "Char, am I getting under your skin?"

She replayed her last comment in her mind and heard how defensive and irritable she had sounded. "I'm sorry," she said, meaning it. "This isn't easy to discuss. I went to Harlan. I . . . trusted him."

"Go on."

She didn't want to go on. She'd made so many mistakes. Why would she want to admit everything to Adam Stiles? He would never, never understand. Betting everything he had on a dream just would never occur to him.

She had begun to wonder why it had never occurred to her. Why in God's name hadn't she been smarter?

"He sold me a share in a top colt he owns," she said, adopting her lawyer's demeanor. "I thought he was being generous. The horse supposedly had Triple Crown potential, and he didn't need to sell me even my relatively small share. If you want to know the truth, at worst I thought he might be carrying a torch for Beth and using me to get back into her life—one reason I was so careful to keep her name out of it. I had no idea he would be so scurrilous as to try to ruin me."

"What happened?" Adam asked quietly.

"In a nutshell, the horse is a dud. Harlan stopped racing him— I have no control over what he does with him. So that's that. My investment's sitting in a stall while his owner laughs up his sleeve over all the money I've lost."

"Sounds like Harlan lost out, too."

"Ha! As you pointed out a few minutes ago, who has my money? *He* does. The only reason he allowed me to buy into that horse was because he knew it was a dud. He misrepresented it to me. His actions were malicious and premeditated, and if I can prove it, I'll take him to court." Char realized she was shouting and lowered her voice. "Bad enough the bastard swindled me, but he also evicted me."

Adam's brow furrowed, but he kept quiet.

Char sighed, figuring she might as well come clean on the whole mess now that she'd started. "He owned the farmhouse I was renting. Writing out that rent check to Harlan Rockwood every month galled me. Not only was I depleting what savings I had left, but it was hell on my pride. I wanted to send him stink bombs, not money. Then he evicted me."

"On what grounds?"

"Any he could make up. I was going to fight, but frankly, I just didn't want to bother."

Adam shifted awkwardly, obviously taking care this time with what he said. "That's when you and Emily moved into the tent."

"On Harlan's property," Char said with some relish.

"He never knew?"

"He'd have called the cops if he had."

"No doubt," Adam said. "Have you talked to him about why the horse didn't perform up to expectations?"

"I've tried. He's not around much, and when he is, I have to go through a million people to get to him—all of whom I've offended at some point or another in the past year."

Adam grinned. "Sweet Charity Bradford offending someone? I can't imagine."

"Okay," she conceded, "so we all know why I'm a lawyer and not a diplomat. But I hate being had. Anyway, Harlan has managed not to return any of my calls, messages, letters, threats—he won't talk."

"So what're you going to do?"

She crossed her arms on her chest, suddenly feeling chilly. "I know things don't look too wonderful, but I'm not a total basket case. I've put money away for Emily's education, and I have almost all of what Beth entrusted with me. What I intend to do now is get *my* money back from that snake Rockwood and get myself back on my feet. In the meantime . . ." She smiled, a self-deprecatory, strangely confident smile, just to show Adam Stiles that if Charity Winnifred Bradford was down, she sure as hell wasn't out. "I'll eat a lot of legumes."

"Not tonight."

His voice was husky, his eyes lost in the shadows of the approaching night, and Char suddenly couldn't ignore the physical reactions she was having to the man. She longed to feel his arms around her. He would be so warm, she thought. So damn solid. For all his lack of imagination, she could trust Adam Stiles.

But all she said was, "No, not tonight."

"MY ONLY QUESTION NOW IS," Adam said halfway through dinner, "why do you want to raise horses?"

They had decided to forgo the kitchen table and made themselves comfortable on the sea of jumbo pillows Char called living room furniture. Her pared-down existence did have a certain appeal: dusting wasn't a big concern. Not since Adam had taken her and Emily out to the restaurant had Char had so much to choose from for dinner. After changing her mind a half-dozen times, she had settled on boneless chicken breasts sauteed in a ginger-and-mandarin-orange sauce, wild rice, steamed fresh spinach and sliced fresh pineapple. Delectable.

Adam's curiosity seemed genuine, and there wasn't even a hint of condemnation in his tone. Char had been listening for it. She recalled his reaction when she had announced over a year ago she was leaving Millbrook and why. "Horses?" he'd sneered. "You've got as much business raising horses as I do." He hadn't believed horses had been a dream for as long as she could remember, a part of the vision she had for herself...a part of the woman she had always intended to become. Adam hadn't swallowed any of that. He had looked at the practical side of her "plan," as she'd called it, and had found it woefully wanting in common sense, a quality of which Char had never been accused of being in short supply.

"And even if you were determined to raise horses," he went on now, "I don't understand why you couldn't have done it in Vermont."

Char set her plate on the floor beside her and leaned back against one of her big, inexpensive pillows. Adam had a sofa, chairs, a television, bookshelves. He had a life. So, she thought miserably, did his children.

"I don't know why horses, why Tennessee, why now—any of it," she said. "I only know coming here was something I needed to do. I couldn't wait any longer. I couldn't keep putting my life on hold."

"That's what Millbrook was to you? Your life on hold?"

"That's what it's always felt like to me, even when I was a kid. I always felt the world was passing me by."

Following her lead, Adam set his plate on the floor beside him. "Your Aunt Millicent's death didn't have anything to do with your decision?"

"It was a factor. I couldn't have done this without the inheritance she left me. And she told me she didn't want me to spend it on anything boring."

Char smiled wistfully, picturing her great-aunt lecturing her from her sickbed on not turning into an old prune. Millicent Bradford had never married, never had any children of her own. She had lived her entire life in Millbrook. A retired elementary teacher, she had practically raised Char. Aunt Mil had been a friend, a sister, a parent—just a damn good woman. More than anyone else, Aunt Mil, independent and frank to a fault, could see past her grandniece's professional demeanor to her warm heart. Her death at eighty-four hadn't been a shock, but it had definitely been a loss.

And also, Char supposed, a catalyst for her move to Tennessee and her disastrous deal with Harlan Rockwood.

"I guess," she went on, "whatever you could say about this past year, it hasn't been boring."

"No," Adam said, but his eyes were on her, studying her with the same intensity—and knowledge, it seemed—he would a prize tree. "You always have to be strong, don't you? For Emily, for everyone. You're not a lawyer just because you're argumentative, which you are. You're a lawyer because you're willing to fight people's battles for them. Showing weakness yourself isn't your style.

"Is that a compliment or an insult?"

"It's an observation. You lost your aunt right about the time you had a few important cases go sour on you, didn't you?"

She stiffened, not wanting to be reminded of those troubled weeks before she'd decided to head south.

Adam didn't wait for her to respond. "I remember thinking life was pretty rough for you at the time, but it seemed you'd bounce back from losing Millicent and those cases just like you bounced back from your divorce, other lost cases, every setback you've ever had in your life. I wished I'd been more sensitive."

Char's eyes narrowed on him. "So I wouldn't have gone off half-cocked and lost all my money?"

"That's not what I meant."

"I'm not in this predicament because of Aunt Millicent or a couple of rotten cases or anything you or anyone else did or didn't say. I'm in it because of me. I grabbed for the brass ring and I missed. Okay? Let's not make more out of it than there is."

"The timing—"

"The timing was perfect." She sprang to her feet, almost tripping on her plate in her rush to get away from Adam's probing gaze. He had never gotten to her like this before. Never! She said abruptly, "You're giving me indigestion. I'm going for a walk."

Adam's voice was mild. "Want some company?"

He looked so damn innocent, as if he hadn't been giving her the third degree the past few minutes. "Will you quit hassling me?"

"Ah, sweet Charity," he said, climbing to his feet. "She can dish it out, but she can't take it."

"I haven't been hassling you!"

He laughed, incredulous. "I suppose you wouldn't call all those wild-goose chases you sent me on last weekend hassling?"

"Of course not."

"Then what were they?"

"A dumb move on my part," she said. "I should have known they'd only whet your appetite to find out what I was really up to." She looked at him, ramrod straight and so damn tall. "But maybe," she added quietly, "I did know."

He smiled. "Maybe you did."

ADAM MADE SURE he walked on Char's right side so that he wouldn't be tempted to grab her hand should the pleasant evening breeze get what was left of his senses. He seldom gave much thought anymore to his missing appendage. In his limited romantic entanglements since Mel's death, he had encountered a wide range of reactions to his disability. There were those women who viewed it with pity and tried to do things for him, to take care of him. Not terribly amusing. Then there were those who were downright squeamish about the whole business and avoided getting near his stump. Understandable at first perhaps, but, again, not terribly amusing. His favorite, however, were those few who insisted a missing hand was downright sexy. That one was definitely amusing, if not altogether credible.

For Char, his disability had always seemed to be one of those things that just was. He had appreciated her matter-of-fact attitude. "Everyone in Millbrook knew one of you Stiles was going to come down out of the hills missing a body part one of these days," she had told him once. "Guess you should be glad you didn't saw off something besides your hand."

Good ol' Char.

She had had the rare good taste not to say better him than either his brother or sister. He had made their lives miserable enough during those guilt-ridden months after Mel's death that if Julian or Beth had been injured, he would have gone straight over the edge. As it was he'd come damn close.

The evening air in central Tennessee was refreshingly cool, a northern high pushing out the last of the clouds and humidity. Adam felt curiously at ease as he and Char walked under the huge oaks that lined the streets of her older neighborhood.

"What do you want me to tell Beth?" he asked, noticing how the night made Char's hair and eyes seem even darker, fathomless.

"Nothing. She'll only be needlessly upset if she finds out I've been had by her ex-husband."

"Upset isn't the word. She'd be down here with her shotgun within twenty-four hours."

Ever the literalist, Char said, "She doesn't own a shotgun."

Adam sighed. "She'd get one."

Char opened her mouth, no doubt to bring up some other impediment to Beth's marching down to Tennessee to enforce a little vigilante justice on wealthy Harlan Rockwood, but she caught herself in time. She angled Adam a look. "You were speaking figuratively," she said. "Then I assume you agree there's no point in putting Beth through all that anger when I don't have to. Her money *is* covered."

"That's not the point," Adam said quietly. He knew he was treading in a mine field now, meddling in the friendship his sister and Char had enjoyed since childhood. "You and Beth went into a bad deal together. Right now you're suffering to protect Beth. In her place would you want that? Wouldn't you want to sink or swim with her?"

"You're asking me to speculate."

"No, I'm asking you to put aside that stubborn Bradford pride and—"

"My pride and my daughter are about all I have left. I don't intend to lose either one."

She shot ahead of him. Adam started to chase after her, but let her go. He understood pride. And he understood parental love. In his own dark days pride and his children had kept him going. They had been his motivator, his reason for regaining some measure of control over his life. They had been a positive force, not a negative, not something that brought him down.

He watched her walking into the stiffening breeze ahead of him and wondered how much alike he and Charity Winnifred really were. It wasn't a thought that would ease his nights.

Neither was the sight of her and what it was doing to his insides. Even mad she possessed a certain unexpected grace, a relentless belief in herself that permeated everything about her, including the way she walked. Her stride was long and quick, her legs able to take her fast pace, her hips—

He'd better not think too much about her hips, he decided with a small grunt.

The breeze caught the ends of her chin-length hair and whipped it into tangles. Before he could stop himself, he was imagining slowly smoothing out the tangles with his fingers.

His pace slackened even as she hit the corner half a block ahead. He hadn't made love with a woman since Mel's death . . . since his accident. Three long years. He had sublimated all his sexual energy into his work. All along he had assumed one of these days, when the time was right, he would want a woman so badly, so obsessively, that no amount of log-sawing would help.

He had just never expected that woman would be Charity Bradford, a no-nonsense attorney who hated Millbrook as much as he loved it. The prospect of any kind of future with her, one in which they both could be happy and fulfilled, was limited, if not laughable. But right now Adam just didn't give a damn about the future, at least not beyond tonight.

Right now all he cared about was how much he wanted her.

She waited for him at the corner. Her shoulders were hunched against the wind, and she shivered, remarking on the dropping temperature. Already accustomed to the brisk New England autumn, Adam barely noticed.

Her eyes, luminous and yet almost black in the darkness, fastened on him in an intense look she could have patented. She asked abruptly, "We're going to do it, aren't we?"

"What?"

But he knew.

Her expression was one that prompted her court-room opponents to slink down in their chairs, but Adam remained focused on her eyes. Still luminous. Passionate. Wanting. And lonely, he realized, feeling a stab of pain for her. So damn lonely.

She half smiled, then answered, "Share a sleeping bag tonight."

"Let's not overanalyze," he said, and tucked a tangled lock of hair behind her ear, feeling the cool softness of her cheek. "Let's just go back to the house and see what happens."

For once she didn't argue.

WHAT HAPPENED BEGAN with an appraisal of the sleeping accommodations. Char had two twin-size cots: one for her and one for Emily. Adam refused to sleep in Emily's cot, on the grounds that he didn't want to disturb the array of stuffed animals she had arranged on her dinosaur sleeping bag. Char wasn't so sure: she had a feeling he had some kind of plan up his sleeve.

Of course, her cot was out altogether.

"Why?" she asked.

He was standing in the doorway, looking into the tiny bedroom where she and Em had set up their beds. Char was in the narrow hallway behind him, near the bathroom and linen closet doors.

He glanced around at her. "I'm going to take your bed while you sleep on the floor?"

"I'll sleep in Em's bed."

He didn't like that, either. Like the Three Bears, Emily would know someone had been sleeping in her bed and would demand an explanation. When she discovered "Uncle" Adam had come to visit while she was out of town, she would be disappointed.

"Then *you* sleep on the floor," Char suggested, her mood something between frustration and anticipation.

She wasn't surprised when that idea didn't meet with his approval, either. Shaking his head, he walked past her into the living room. She followed. The house was absolutely still, the shadows, the quiet, the slight chill all a reminder that it was nightfall.

Adam surveyed the living room, frowning. "You don't have any rugs," he pointed out, "and my sleeping bag's fairly thin. It'd be damn uncomfortable sleeping on the floor."

Char settled against the doorway, arms folded over her chest, one leg bent. "There's still time to check into a hotel. Or you can try the old doghouse out back."

He ignored her sarcasm. "I do have an idea."

"No kidding."

"I noticed you have a thick sleeping bag. We could open it up and spread it on the floor as a makeshift mattress and use mine as a blanket."

She looked right at him. "That means sleeping together."

He looked back. "Uh-huh. It does."

Her lighthearted, teasing mood lasted only a few more seconds until she could feel the heat in his eyes, could feel it bubbling in her blood. They were finished playing games. They weren't talking about a couple of old pals arm-wrestling for the hell of it. They were talking about spending the night together.

"Adam, I don't want to ruin our friendship."

He laughed softly, coming toward her. "What friendship?" he asked, slipping his arms around her.

The strength of his chest against her felt so good, better even than she had hoped. All evening, Char thought, she had vacillated between feeling totally at ease with Adam Stiles and wanting to put him on the next plane headed north. Now any feelings of uneasiness seemed so long ago, so distant. She wanted to be exactly where she was. He went on, quietly, wryly, "You and I have tolerated each other for years. We haven't been enemies—but friends? Come on. Seems to me we must have just been waiting for lightning to strike."

Lightning had struck all right, Char thought. Even her toes felt singed. His mouth found hers, opened at once, until she felt teeth and tongue, until she began to burn. Ignited, she slid her hands around his back and drew him toward her, pressing her breasts against the solid wall of his chest. He pressed back. She could feel the hardness of him. They were throbbing, burning.

They made short work of their bedding arrangements. And their clothes. Char pulled the shades, Adam shook open the sleeping bags. They both helped with each other's clothes. They were a giant bonfire that would burn for days. They were two people consumed with a flaming passion that had appeared as suddenly, as irrevocably, as a bolt of lightning on a barn filled with dry hay.

Naked—sleek and hot—they fell atop both sleeping bags, Adam easing Char onto him. They kissed for a long time, deeply, touching and stroking, wanting. Char felt herself being transported into another place, another time . . . away from her problems, her doubts. It was as if the heat of their longing enveloped Adam and herself and kept the world at bay.

Then all at once she felt herself plunging back to reality.

All at once there wasn't just the present. There wasn't just heat and longing and *now*.

She raised herself off Adam's chest. "What about tomorrow?"

"We'll sleep late," he said, running his hand along her side, from her hip to her shoulder, "and have one hell of a breakfast."

"And you'll head back to Vermont."

His thick eyebrows drew closer together. "I have two kids—"

"I know." Her heart was drumming so hard she thought he must hear it. "I'm not complaining. But, Adam, what are we starting?"

He gently pushed her hair back behind her ear, then eased her off him as he raised himself on one elbow. "I don't know and I won't pretend I do. Char, neither one of us has a crystal ball."

"Yes, but . . ." She licked her lips, wondering if she were going to end up as big a damn fool about romance as she was about horses. "We're levelheaded people, Adam. I may have lost everything on a dirty horse deal, but that's an aberration. And when it comes to men—"

"You try to control what you can't control," he finished for her.

"You're the same way with women."

He didn't argue.

"We haven't had a proper date yet," she blundered on, "and here we are in bed together.

"Sometimes things just happen."

"They *can't*. Not with me, not anymore."

Adam sighed, rolling up into a sitting position. Char took due note of his flat stomach, the hard muscles of his shoulders and arms, but quenched any renewed sparks.

"Char, you've known me your entire life. It's not as if we're a couple of strangers who just met."

"I know. Maybe it'd be easier if we were."

"Yeah, maybe. Look—" He raked his hand through his hair. "If you want to stay up half the night talking, would you mind if we got up? It's been a while for me, and speaking of control . . ."

"Oh." Char could feel herself flushing from head to toe. "Oh! Adam, I'm sorry."

"We haven't done anything to be sorry about," he pointed out wryly.

"Well, we could finish—"

"For my sake? I'd rather be celibate than accept charity sex—no pun intended."

Char backed off the bedding and stood up quickly, the rush of cool night air on her overheated skin having a devastating effect. It was rather like tossing gasoline on hot coals. There was no question she was aroused . . . that she desperately wanted this man.

But that was the whole point, wasn't it? She didn't want to act out of desperation.

She couldn't.

"I need to get my life in order," she mumbled, noticing Adam's eyes on her pebbled nipples, "before I get involved."

He nodded curtly. "Okay."

She was relieved that he wasn't pressing her for a better explanation. And also a little annoyed. "That's it? Just 'okay'?"

"We can talk in the morning. Char, I can see you're ambivalent about what's going on between us."

"I'm not. I want what's happening to happen, just not right now. No, that's not true, either. I'm glad you're here. I hated the idea of being alone this weekend." She sighed, her shoulders sagging. "You're right. I am ambivalent. But doesn't that bug you just a little?"

He gave her a dry look. "'Bug' isn't the word I'd use."

"Then what?"

"Frustrate."

"You mean you're not just going to roll over and go to sleep?"

"Hardly."

She grabbed her shirt and pulled it over her head. "Good."

Adam shifted onto his stomach, his torso raised as he looked up at her. "And you?"

"I'll sleep in Em's bed. One thing about a dinosaur bag," she said, "I'll bet it eradicates all thoughts of sex."

Fortunately or unfortunately, it didn't.

7

AS HE LISTENED to the shower pounding on Char's lithe body from the kitchen, Adam came to the conclusion something strange was in the Tennessee air. He wasn't acting normal. Wanting to make love to a woman was normal enough, he supposed. But wanting to make love to *Char*? Millbrook's sharp-eyed ex-lawyer? Harlan Rockwood's latest victim? A woman who would rather live in a tent than admit failure?

No, wanting to make love to Char wasn't normal. It was madness.

He imagined the hot water streaming down the silken skin of her back.

Lord.

Charity Winnifred Bradford, he reminded himself, wasn't the easiest person in the world to be around.

She lived in Tennessee, a thousand miles from Vermont.

She hated Millbrook.

Adam jumped up from the folding chair at her sawhorse kitchen table. The woman was in such a predicament—one she would, of course, insist she get herself out of on her own—that she didn't even have a decent chair. She *owned* several, but they were all in storage in her despised hometown.

But the uncomfortable chair wasn't why he was uneasy, and Adam knew it. He was uneasy—*damn* uneasy—because a night's sleep hadn't changed a thing.

Because, awakening this morning, he had wanted Char as much as he had the night before.

Worse.

He dragged out her cast-iron skillet and slammed it down on her stove.

Would she never finish with her shower?

He could feel his mouth on her hot, wet skin. He could taste her sweet, soapy kiss. He could feel the slap of her wet hair against his shoulder.

Then he heard the water shut off and exhaled in relief.

His relief was short-lived. Another image took form in his mind. He could see her drying off with a soft, warm towel . . . as soft and warm as her body.

He tore open the refrigerator and dug around until he found the pound of Tennessee sausages they had bought yesterday. His fingers were shaking. Hell, all he needed to do was hack off the top of a finger.

Calm down, my man.

But it had been *three years.*

Down the hall in the bathroom, Charity began to hum.

"Char, goddamn it, are you deliberately trying to torture me?"

"Huh?"

So innocent.

"Never mind," he yelled.

Using his left forearm and right hand, he deftly got the wrapping off the sausages and sliced off eight fat chunks. His frustration with working one-handed had lessened with time and experience, but there were still moments, if increasingly rare, when he yelled and threw things and generally locked horns with his disability.

Generally, unless he was reminded, he no longer gave it much thought.

He laid the sausages in the skillet and hunted up the pancake mix they had also picked up on their shopping excursion. Ordinarily he made pancakes from scratch, but he didn't want to take any chances with Char's supply of cooking utensils. From his survey of her kitchen, he would say that had been smart thinking. She would blame her subsistence living, he supposed, but even back in Vermont, with a well-equipped kitchen at her disposal, Char had never put herself out when it came to cooking.

All he had to do to the pancake mix was add an egg and milk, which he did while the sausages began to sizzle. He would have breakfast ready in no time. Food, he hoped, would help the raw ache gnawing on his insides. At the rate he was going, they would be finished by eleven . . . and his flight didn't leave until after nine tonight.

He held the bowl with his forearm and beat the batter hard.

If Char thought he was going to spend the entire day locked up in this tiny house with her, she'd better think again. Being an uninvited guest permitted her to subject him to only so much torture.

The bathroom door creaked open, and in a moment Char came into the kitchen in her ratty, outrageously sexy white chenille bathrobe. She dropped into a chair. Her cheeks were rosy. Her hair was bundled up in a tangerine towel. She had nothing on her feet.

Adam figured it would take two seconds, maybe three, to untie her robe and just let it fall from her shoulders.

"Good morning," he said, quickly turning back to his sausages.

"Morning."

The sausages were cooking fast now. Since Char didn't have a griddle, he would have to clean out the skillet before he could cook the pancakes. He didn't mind. Better that he should keep busy.

Last night had opened doors he had shut and locked years ago. Even before Mel's death he had given up on personal happiness for himself. His kids were healthy, his work was satisfying. That was enough. A man, he had assumed, shouldn't ask for too much in life; it was all too easy to lose what you had. Romantic love was a myth, he had decided. What he and Mel had had for most of their marriage was what most people had: a relationship built on conditions, in their case, lots of conditions.

He *had* loved Mel. The passion, the infatuation, the needing—that was all a distant memory now, and had been for a long, long time. If he had wanted to work out their problems before her death, it had been a desire born more of stubbornness than enduring love. He had never dreamed about Mel, had never fantasized about her. He wasn't a romantic soul, he had concluded. He wasn't a dreamer.

Last night, however, he had dreamed about Charity Bradford.

He had fantasized about her.

He *knew* what making love to her would be like. And he knew that knowing wasn't enough. Sooner or later, it was something they were going to have to experience together.

Right now, looking at Char, feeling his raw, pounding desire for her, he would bet on sooner rather than later. He sensed her thoughts were drifting in the same direction, but he remembered last night. That they would be able to pull back again was expecting too much for their beleaguered bodies, but he didn't want to do anything they, or she, would regret.

"The sausages smell great," she said, sounding awkward for smooth-talking Char Bradford. "Do I have time to get dressed before we eat?"

Adam's mouth went dry. "You'd better take time."

She managed a weak smile. "Yeah, I guess so. Frankly, Adam, this whole thing feels weird."

He arched her a look, but kept quiet.

"You know."

"Uh-uh. I don't."

"Your . . . um . . . wanting me like that. It's weird."

Weird? Adam stabbed a sausage with a fork and flipped it out onto a paper bag to drain. Weird, he thought. The woman was going to drive him mad. He glanced around at her, a flush spreading from her cheeks to the smooth skin exposed where her robe was wrapped loosely above her breasts.

"How come weird?" he asked in as neutral a voice as he could manage. It wasn't very neutral.

She lifted her shoulders and let them fall in an exaggerated movement that only made her seem more nonplussed, which nobody back in Millbrook would believe. She said, "The name Adam Stiles and control have always gone hand in hand. But last night . . ."

Her voice trailed off, and Adam got all the sausages out of the skillet before turning back to face her. "Char," he said dryly, "last night should have confirmed, not undermined, any reputation for control."

She sprang to her feet. Adam took a perverse pleasure in knowing he was getting to her, that it wasn't just her getting to him, but he hid his grin from her by grabbing the skillet and emptying the fat into an old coffee can. He heard Char mumble something about being back in a few minutes, then the sound of her bare feet padding on the hardwood floor. He assumed she was getting dressed. A wise decision. In a few minutes she would have seen just how weird and out of control he could get.

He sighed. What did she take him for? Did the women of Millbrook gossip about the ascetic one-handed sawyer up on the river? Had they come to the conclusion he was no longer interested in sex?

Weird.

Control.

Adam had never been a man who concerned himself with other people's opinion of him. What his reputation was or wasn't had never crossed his mind. This, however, was different.

It was insulting was what it was.

How could Char be surprised he wanted her so much when she had damn little idea, really, of how much he *did* want her? He *had* controlled himself last night.

He called back to the bedroom, "You know, just because I'm a one-handed widower doesn't mean it should surprise you I can still kiss a woman!"

He couldn't make out her response, but it sounded argumentative. He cleaned out the skillet, and by the time he had it back on the stove, heating up for the pancakes, Char came bounding out from the bedroom. She had on jeans and a teal sweatshirt and her hair was all over the place.

"You are such a jackass," she told him.

Now they were on firm ground, Adam thought. Char being straightforward and crabby he understood. Her flushing and mumbling threw him off. He said mildly, "Just trying to figure you out, Char."

She crossed her arms over her chest, prosecutorial style. "I wasn't talking about you wanting a woman in general being weird, but me in particular."

He stirred the pancake batter. "Why should that be weird?"

"I'm not your type."

"What's my type?"

"I wouldn't presume to say, but if I were it, you'd have noticed me sooner, seeing as you've known me since I was in a cradle."

He laughed. "Thought I'd wait until you were toilet-trained before I made any moves on you."

"Damn it, you know what I'm talking about!"

He turned on the faucet, wet his fingers and flipped droplets of water onto the heating skillet. The water danced and then evaporated. Perfect. He ladled in batter for one large pancake.

"I could say the same thing about you," he pointed out, "except that it occurs to me maybe you haven't 'noticed' me. I'm the one who's barged into your life. Char, are you trying to tell me I'm shoving myself on you and you'd just as soon I backed off? If so, out with it."

She shook her head tightly, and Adam quickly set down the ladle, careful to hide the rush of relief he felt. He wasn't sure he was ready to confront his own feelings about Char yet, never mind have her confront them. Being a repressed Yankee—never minding that such a stereotype would annoy her—she didn't articulate her feelings any more easily than he did.

Sighing, she said, "No, that's not what I'm trying to tell you."

Adam grabbed a spatula and kept his eye on the cooking pancake. "Then are you trying to tell me that our attraction to each other has more to do with raging hormones and a very small house than anything deeper?"

"You could say that."

"Then I suggest," he said, watching bubbles form on the top of the pancake, "we eat breakfast and get out of this house for the afternoon."

"What about our hormones?" she asked, a welcome touch of humor in her tone.

He looked around at her and grinned. "Let them rage."

AND RAGE THEY DID.

Thinking it would be safe there, Char took Adam to Opryland. The summer crowds had thinned somewhat, but the popular amusement park and home of the world-famous Grand Ole Opry was still jam-packed. The weather was clear and warm, and country and western music, which always seemed to reenergize Char, was playing everywhere. After their ride over to Opryland in the close confines of her car, she welcomed anything that would help clear her head, and ease her aching awareness of Adam.

He, naturally, only went to amusement parks for the sake of his kids. Even so, he never rode any of the rides. "Always seemed like a waste of time," he said to Char as she stood back and let him pay for her ticket. It wounded her pride, but she was down to twenty-three days to come up with next month's rent. Anyway, she'd pay him back every cent.

"Well, that's why we're here," she told him.

"To waste time?" He shook his head as they headed into the park. "No way. We're here to distract ourselves."

She angled a look at him. "Think it'll work?"

He met her gaze, his eyes bright in the noontime sun. "Not a chance."

Char suddenly felt warm . . . wanted. She hadn't felt that way in a devilishly long time. Needed, yes. By her daughter, her clients. But not wanted. Without thinking, she hooked her right arm through Adam's left arm. She hardly noticed the absence of his hand.

"Well, we'll just have to give it a try."

They tried.

Char dragged him onto all her favorite rides: the Screamin' Delta Demon—Adam didn't scream; the Flume Zoom—he didn't even get wet; the Mill River Scream—he did get wet, but he still didn't scream. He looked a little out of place in the lines, a stolid, one-handed Yankee in a work shirt and jeans always checking around for stray kids. "I feel like a nine-year-old," he'd mutter from time to time. Char accused him of feeling guilty because he was spending a Sunday afternoon doing something so useless as riding down a made-up waterfall and getting wet on purpose. He ought to be looking after his kids or cutting wood or fixing dinners for the next week. Doing something productive.

"That's not true," he said.

"Before you decided to come down here and meddle in my life," she persisted, "what did you have planned for this afternoon?"

"I don't know."

"You do, too."

He scowled at her. "Okay. I was going to clean the chimney."

It was all Char could do to hold in a victorious hoot. Instead she said, as if in a courtroom, "I rest my case."

"It needs cleaning before winter."

"Of course."

"Char—"

"Adam, you are *such* a Yankee."

He bit off his next comment and climbed into their seat for the Cannonball, her favorite maniacal ride. "My idea of a good time," he grumbled, "isn't getting turned upside down on a damn roller coaster."

"No, cleaning chimneys is."

The look he gave her was a scorcher and all she needed to realize the afternoon wasn't distracting him at all. Not letting up, he said, "Hardly."

Fortunately the notorious ride began to move.

As they were being whipped around, Char thought she heard Adam give a yell of pure abandon. Since everyone else—including she—was screaming, she couldn't be sure. But she thought it was his purely Vermont voice yelling as they went into the second wild upside-down turn.

Afterward, he suggested Goo-goo Cluster ice-cream cones.

Opryland or self-denial, she decided, were having their effect.

The Grizzly River Rampage ended any fading notion she might have had that they could find, even for just a few hours, an innocuous middle ground between being a couple of people who had always just tolerated each other and potential lovers. The ride was a drencher: a giant inner tube floated down a river in manufactured white water and under a waterfall. It wasn't scary or nauseating. It was just wet.

They both got soaked to the skin.

The sight of a fully clothed Adam Stiles, the hardcase president of Mill Brook Post & Beam, dripping wet was more than Char could handle. She hadn't laughed so hard in months.

Adam, however, wasn't nearly as amused. At first Char thought he was going to complain she hadn't sufficiently warned him about just how wet he might get, but he didn't say a word. Then a cool late-afternoon breeze struck her and his arm brushed up against her. Char almost lost her balance. With the wind on her wet skin and his touch, she had the delicious sensation of feelings hot and cold at the same time. Her shirt was matted against her breasts, outlining their shape in detail, but before she could cover up she saw that Adam had already taken due notice of her hardened nipples.

She also saw that their afternoon out had no more distracted him than it had her.

"The sun'll dry us in a few minutes," she said, her voice raspy. "Want to head back? I know a great place for barbecue on the way."

They were still damp when they arrived at the barbecue place, so they decide to get their sandwiches and coleslaw to go. Char loftily insisted on paying. But she wasn't hungry when they got back to her house. She felt clammy, there was a slight chill to the air and Adam still had a couple of hours before he had to be at the airport.

Char excused herself and slipped into the shower, turning the water on extra hot. Maybe consciously or unconsciously they had planned it this way, she thought. Or maybe it was just a coincidence. She supposed it didn't matter. Whatever her motives or his, here they were. And she wasn't going to let the weekend slip away. She wasn't going to let Adam slip away.

She wasn't going to wait for tomorrow's regrets.

When she joined him back in the living room, he had put on fresh clothes and had shaken his sleeping bag out and spread it neatly on the floor so that he could roll it up for travel.

He scanned her bathrobe and bare feet. "You dress like this for dinner every night?"

"Not every night." She suddenly felt self-conscious and dropped onto a giant pillow. "I'll get dressed in a little bit. You can use the shower now, if you want."

"Let me finish with this—"

"That's okay. I'll finish it for you. You go ahead."

Eyeing her with open suspicion, Adam climbed to his feet. Char had no clear idea of what she was doing; she had no plan, no goal. All she knew was that when she started her new job tomorrow morning, when Adam was back in Vermont sawing logs, she didn't want to be confronted with a slew of regrets. She wanted to give whatever they had percolating between them at least half a chance to boil over.

"All right," Adam said with a slight shrug, and headed for the shower.

Char cursed silently.

The bathroom door closed with a firm thud, and Adam began to whistle. She heard the shower come on. The man wasn't going to make this easy on her, was he? She flopped back against another pillow and kicked out her legs in front of her so that she was lying flat on her back staring at the ceiling. It needed paint. *She* needed something, too. A total overhaul, probably. She had to be crazy wanting a thickheaded, dull Yankee like

Adam Stiles. *Only* Adam would have left her sitting there inches from his spread-out sleeping bag and gone in to take that shower.

Unless . . .

Char shot upright and glared down the hall toward the bathroom.

Unless he wanted her to be absolutely, positively, one hundred percent sure that she would have no regrets . . . that she wouldn't pull back in the last second as she had last night. Maybe he was giving her that one final chance to come to her senses.

Except she wasn't out of her mind, she realized. She was stone-cold rational and knew—*knew*—she couldn't let Adam slip away. She didn't have a crystal ball. She didn't know what would happen to them. But did that matter?

Not right now it didn't.

She climbed to her feet and trotted down the hall to the bathroom. Just what was the etiquette for this sort of thing? Should she knock first? Barge in? Whisper something seductive?

"Oh, rot."

"Char!" Adam yelled, as if she were down in the back forty. "You got a dry towel somewhere around here?"

Perfect.

There was one under the sink, of course, but no need to tell him that. "Hang on a second. I'll have to hand one in."

That would alert him to her opening the door, and she could take her cue from whether he was exercising modesty or not. Snatching the towel through the barely cracked door would suggest she should just go and put supper on. Allowing her to walk into the bathroom and hand the towel to him in the shower would suggest she might want to join him.

She peeled off the towel she had wrapped over her wet hair and cracked open the door.

Nothing.

Her heart pounding, she hung the towel on one finger and stretched out her arm as she poked her head into the tiny bathroom.

Adam wasn't exercising modesty.

Sleek and dark and stark naked, he was standing in front of the tub with his eyes on the door.

"You're not even wet," Char blurted.

"Didn't want to parade through the house dripping while I hunted up a towel."

"I see. Well, here you go."

He caught the towel handily, his eyes never leaving her. Then he nodded to the old pedestal sink, where she had left her comb. "You want to comb out your hair before the tangles dry?"

"I won't bother you?"

"Guess that's up to you."

With an unself-consciousness Char would expect in a locker room, Adam slung the towel over the curtain bar and climbed into the tub. The steam from the hot water escaped when he drew back the curtain, hitting her full in the face.

"Come in or get out," Adam said as he pulled the curtain shut. "You're creating a draft with the door open."

The opaque shower curtain meant he was at least out of immediate view. *I do need to comb my hair*, Char thought, quickly shutting the door behind her. She could analyze her situation interminably. Adam would freeze, her hair would dry in tangles. Best just to close the damn door and *then* think. Sticking around a few minutes didn't necessarily mean she and Adam would end up making love on the bathroom floor. There wasn't enough room, anyway. Even if they scrunched up . . .

She saw how red her face was in the steamy mirror and abandoned that line of thinking.

The comb, she thought. *Grab the comb and get busy.*

It seemed so natural, combing her hair at the sink while Adam took a shower. She could hear him lathering up a washcloth.

"There's enough hot water?" she asked, raising her voice above the noise of the shower.

"Plenty."

If she hadn't known Adam as well as she did, his reply would have sounded like a growl to her . . . a growl of frustration, of wanting. They were torturing each other. She tore the comb through her hair, tears springing in her eyes as she ripped through tangles. Was she out of her mind? She shouldn't have come into the bathroom. *Let the man shower in peace, for heaven's sake.*

Suddenly the shower was off. The tiny bathroom was silent; Char stood motionless at the sink.

"You still in here?" he asked.

"Yes." She put down her comb; she was finished, anyway. "I'll go—"

"Don't."

He pushed open the shower curtain and came to her, sweeping his arms around her before she could think to protest. Not that she would have. This was what she wanted; this was why she had delivered him the towel in the first place. He had left it dangling from the rod. His body was wet and hot and hard. Her robe grew damp as its worn chenille absorbed the water from his chest and abdomen, aroused her almost as much as his touch.

"We've waited a long time for this," he said. "Too damn long."

His mouth found hers. She groaned softly, opened her lips, welcoming, urging. She could feel him burning with her, could feel herself becoming wax melting around a hot flame. Drops of water dripped from his hair onto her cheek, then down her throat and over her breasts, singeing her.

The loose tie of her robe gave way, suddenly exposing her nipples to the sleek muscles and prickly hairs of his chest. She gasped at the sheer ferocity of her want. Was she mad? Could he possibly want her as much as she did him?

Then, before she was aware of what was happening, he drew her tighter to him. His tongue probed deeply into her mouth. She could feel the tension in his muscles, suddenly knew that the kisses, the burning, the touching were only a small hint of how much he wanted her. He was holding back, straining against a longing that she suddenly realized was every bit as great as her own.

The robe fell off her shoulders, and he hungrily tore it the rest of the way off and cast it onto the floor. His mouth came off hers for that instant. She tried to catch her breath, but saw his eyes, dusky and absolutely focused on what he wanted. Before she could gulp a breath, he took one of her nipples in his mouth and teased it between his teeth until she cried out with the heat that engulfed her. She stroked his shoulders, ran her fingers into his wet hair... felt the heat and strain of hanging on in him.

She was gasping. "We should go in the other room…"

"No time."

"There's no room—"

"There's room." His smile was ravaged, aching. "Trust me."

Unable to delay another second, she gave in and dropped to the floor. She could have been on cold, bare tile for all she would have cared, but the handwoven mat she had carted with her from Vermont and her tattered cast-off robe were cushion, and warmth, enough.

He was on his knees, just his mouth touching hers.

"Don't stop," she whispered. She slid her hands down his arms, shot over to his waist and eased them over his smooth, hard hips, pulling him onto her. "Just don't stop."

His eyes searched hers for a moment. "Never."

And he came into her with a single thrust that was so hard, so fast, so exquisite she almost erupted then. She was aware of yelling, but what she didn't know.

"This is perfect," he whispered, moving slowly inside her, still holding his breath. "Perfect."

She made her agreement known with her body, and he groaned, his thrusts going harder, deeper, faster. He no longer held back. Within seconds the contained fire they had built between them, hot and wonderful, was a wildfire raging out of control. It consumed everything in its path—inhibitions, self-restraint, old animosities, remoteness. Everything that had kept them at bay was left charred, like the blackened forest after a fire, to be replaced with new, fragile growth.

They didn't speak afterward, but walked hand in hand into the living room, where they made love again, cushioned by sleeping bags and pillows. They went slowly this time, exploring, inventing, laughing, teasing. They were like two seeds, Char thought, blowing across the blackened landscape, looking for a place to land, spread roots, grow and flower.

"I've never known anyone like you," Adam told her as he stroked her hair.

And she smiled, because, of course, there was only one Adam Stiles and if all the world didn't know it, all of Vermont did. Especially her.

They showered again, together, and ate their barbecue sandwiches as she and, in turn, Adam, told silly and outrageous stories about things their kids had done, things they themselves had done when they were growing up together in small-town Vermont.

Later, when they were dressed and ready to leave for the airport, Adam brushed a finger through her hair. "No regrets?"

Char shook her head without hesitation. "None."

"Same here. Char, when I get back to Vermont—"

"No, Adam." She cut him off gently, but could feel her chest tightening at thoughts of the future, of reality. "Let's not think about tomorrow right now. I'm starting a new job. I've got unfinished business here. You've got a business to help run back home. We can't promise how we'll feel, what we'll do. No promises, okay?"

He studied her for a moment, his eyes more green than blue now, like dark, gleaming emeralds. Then he nodded. But Char could tell he had already made up his mind about how he felt, what he would do. He just wasn't telling her, and that, for now, was what she wanted.

At the airport he did kiss her goodbye, for a long enough time that people began to stare. They both noticed and laughed, embarrassed, for public displays of affection weren't in their background.

"Next time we'll take Abby and David and Em to Opryland with us," Adam said.

Next time. "Right."

And Char's knees were rubbery and her mouth dry when she left Adam to board his plane and headed down to the gate where Emily, little world-traveler that she was, was arriving in an hour. Suddenly she couldn't wait to see her daughter. She was her reality, her anchor, her reason for not sinking into despair or doing something to Harlan Rockwood that would land her in jail, or even saying to hell with it all and running after Adam. For Emily's sake she had to remain whole. She couldn't give in to desperation. She couldn't let Adam Stiles rescue her from herself.

Emily came out of the jetway in a frilly new dress and with a big grin on her cherubic face. Char couldn't tell whether it was with relief or a touch of regret that the flight attendant returned her charge to her mother. On her last visit with her father, Emily had learned she could ask for extra bags of peanuts.

Mother and daughter headed off together, arm in arm. Char gave one final glance toward the gate where she'd left Adam. He would be thirty thousand feet up in the air by now, on his way back home. Char wanted him back down on terra firma with her, in Nashville. She knew that much. But she also knew that she had to get her life sorted out on her own, and having Adam Stiles around wouldn't allow her to do that. He was a man of action. Asking him not to act was like asking him not to breathe. It would be easier on him, she hoped, being back in Vermont.

"First things first," she said to herself, and smiled at Emily in her god-awful new dress.

She would go on.

8

ADAM ARRIVED BACK HOME in a stormy mood that persisted through the week. He kept to himself and assumed no one else noticed that his second trip to Tennessee hadn't agreed with him any more than his first one. With Char on his mind, he stayed away from the mill's huge saws. He burrowed in at his desk, making overdue phone calls and digging into paperwork. He let Julian and Beth handle employee relations and outside visitors, explaining that he had too much else on his mind right now to deal with people directly. It wasn't long before his two siblings had a fair idea that the "much else" had virtually nothing to do with Mill Brook Post & Beam.

Julian was the first to call his older brother onto the mat about his mood. Newly married and himself swamped with projects, such as the renovation of the prestigious, now-defunct Millbrook Academy for Boys, Julian wasn't one to concern himself with his brother's occasional spells of brooding. Adam sometimes withdrew from the people around him. Julian understood that need. For him to notice and comment on his brother's mood, Adam knew, meant it had to be out of the realm of what Julian would consider normal—which meant most everyone else was probably steering clear of the president of Mill Brook Post & Beam altogether.

Julian lowered himself into the wooden chair near Adam's desk in a far corner of the large, open office floor of the eighteenth-century sawmill. "Morning," he said.

Adam grunted without looking up from a stack of orders.

"Busy day ahead?"

"No more than usual."

"Good," Julian said. "Then we can let Beth mind the shop and get some lunch in town."

Adam still didn't look up. "No time."

He heard Julian sigh. "You haven't left the mill since you got back from Tennessee. You work here all day, then go home—"

Setting down his pencil, Adam turned in his chair. "I'm aware of what I do."

Julian didn't flinch under his brother's relentless stare. Adam's reputation for unapproachability had never had any noticeable effect on either his brother or his sister. Or Charity Bradford. She had always been annoyingly unique among his nonrelations in that regard.

Adam swore under his breath, tensing. Char again. All week he had worked at repressing any thought of her—unsuccessfully. She was always there, hovering in his thoughts. Time hadn't made putting her out of his mind any easier.

"You're a grouch, Adam," Julian said casually, stretching out his legs as if settling himself for a long chat. "Char's always pushed you to the edge, but now maybe she's pushed you over. What'd she do this time?"

Adam scowled. "Don't you have work to do?"

"Lunch," Julian said, snapping his legs back and rising. "Noon. I'll drive."

Not bothering to argue, Adam impatiently waved Julian off and returned to his work. He wasn't having lunch with his brother or anyone else. He would have a sandwich at his desk, as he had had every day this week. If Julian wanted to join him, fine. They could discuss the academy renovations or any other business. If he brought up Adam's bad mood, Adam would boot him back to his own desk. But he wasn't going out.

And he sure as hell wasn't discussing Charity Bradford.

When Adam made his position clear at noon, Julian didn't make a scene or even argue. Instead he sent Beth in. She lacked any of Julian's subtlety. Sitting on one end of Adam's desk, she gave him a once-over.

"What the hell's wrong with you?" she demanded. "The whole damn town knows you're not fit to live with these days."

Adam wheeled his chair back and said nothing. His sister was prone to exaggeration. His desire to pull himself back into himself for a while didn't effect his relationship with his children: Abby and David received his full attention, while aware he had other things on his mind. Unexplained things. Like Char Bradford, hardheaded, broke, the ex-lawyer who hated Millbrook. Like her war with his sister's ex-husband. Like how much Adam wanted to fly back to Tennessee and fight her battles for her. Every minute he had to resist the temptation to pick up the phone and dial his travel agent. But Abby and David, as attuned to his human complexities as he was to theirs, gave him space and didn't pester him too much with questions they had no business asking.

Unlike their uncle and aunt.

"Something happen in Tennessee you don't want to tell me?" Beth asked.

Lots. Adam narrowed his eyes at his younger sister, a sturdy, hotheaded woman as action-oriented as either of her brothers. The thought of her energy left half the residents gasping for air and the other half shaking their heads in wonder. A nonconformist and a devilishly hard worker, she had the capacity to skewer men in their chairs with just one look. Her brief marriage to Harlan Rockwood had left her cynical on the subject of romantic love. Adam had no intention of bringing up with her the dreams of Char that had haunted his nights all week. Beth would only blame some chemical imbalance in his system—hormones. And howl with laughter at the idea of her equally hardheaded best friend having such an effect on her brother, whom Beth had always relied upon for being as unromantic as she.

"You and Julian are making a mountain out of a molehill," Adam told her with more patience than he felt. Given a choice, he would rather rile Julian than Beth. "I have a lot of work to do. If you two quit bugging me, I might get it done."

Beth didn't budge. "You told me Char's fine. She didn't just talk you into telling me that, did she?"

"No."

In fact, he had talked himself into reporting back to Beth such an outright lie. Of course Char wasn't fine. She was broke. She was going after one of Tennessee's wealthiest men. She was *nuts* was what she was. But Adam didn't want to come between his sister and her friend. In hindsight he should have never gotten involved in their schemes in the first place. Now he sure as hell didn't want to be the one who told Harlan Rockwood's ex-wife that he had swindled her best friend out of everything she had...including, no doubt not incidentally, twenty grand that belonged to Beth Stiles herself.

Adam wasn't worried that Beth would take out her emotions on Char: she didn't think like that. No, she would go after Harlan herself. Adam knew it, and so, probably, did Char. Char would have her reasons— protecting Beth, solving her problems herself. Adam had his. It didn't make much sense to him, but the fact was, he liked Harlan enough as a person not to sic Beth on him. He was hoping, perhaps naively, that Harlan's disastrous business dealings with Char could be explained and resolved to their mutual satisfaction without involving Beth. Adam didn't want to defend Harlan without all the facts, but he didn't want to lynch him, either.

Or turn his fire-eating sister on the poor bastard.

Such thinking, of course, wouldn't get him far with either woman. Neutrality wasn't something Beth Stiles nor Char Bradford wanted to encounter when dealing with Harlan Rockwood.

"Adam," Beth said, "I haven't heard from Char all week. You won't talk. You sit over here like a damn thundercloud waiting to burst. What's going on?"

"If you want to know what's going on with Char, talk to her. There's nothing going on with me."

Beth scoffed. "You went back to Tennessee for the expressed purpose of finding out what Char was up to. Did you?"

"Talk to Char yourself."

"So you found out something and won't tell me."

"I'm not going to come between you two. I don't know what the hell was wrong with me that I even got involved in this mess in the first place. I'm out of it, okay? Whatever you and Char have going is your business. I've got work to do."

"Fine," Beth said huffily, cutting him off.

Adam sighed and looked at his only sister with as much patience as he could muster up. It wasn't much. "I'm in a no-win situation, Beth. Cut me some slack."

She gave him a look that suggested she would willingly cut him something besides slack—namely a noose—and flounced off.

Adam gave up and yelled to his brother. "Okay, damn it, you win. Get me the hell out of here. I don't care where we go—just don't mention Tennessee, horses or Charity Bradford."

Julian grinned, and Adam realized that he had just confirmed that it was precisely Tennessee, horses and Charity Bradford that were bothering him. He didn't bother telling his brother that Tennessee and horses were way down on his list. Mostly it was Charity Bradford.

CHAR LASTED at her new job exactly four days. She considered that something of an achievement: she had wanted to quit after four hours. Helping people choose lipsticks and hide the bags under their eyes made her irritable, and she hadn't gotten up on Monday morning in that great a mood to begin with. Too much obsessing about Adam Stiles. As if she didn't have other things to think about and didn't know better than most just what she was getting into, falling for that one-handed Yankee sawyer.

She would tell her customers, "Here, take the poppy-red," instead of letting them arrive at the decision themselves, and even when they did choose, she would argue: "No—that shade of plum will make you look like a corpse."

Her colleagues behind the cosmetic counter instructed her on the art of tact, never her long suit. She was used to being straightforward with people and being able to get away with saying more than she sometimes should say. She wasn't mean. She was just . . . blunt. Her penchant for speaking her mind in not always the most diplomatic of ways had never hurt her in her law practice. People—or at least the citizens of her corner of Vermont—responded to a lawyer who said what was what.

That approach didn't necessarily work in selling cosmetics. The idea was to lead people into appropriate colors and show them techniques that would highlight their best features. But if they wanted plum, her colleagues would tell Char, and plum made 'em look sick, sell 'em the plum.

She didn't quit. There was still the problem of the rent to keep in mind, and Adam's groceries wouldn't last forever. Char figured she was learning lessons in humility, patience, what made women feel more attractive and the art of selling a product. But biting her tongue didn't come easily, and apparently she wasn't succeeding all that well.

She was fired on Thursday afternoon.

Her boss, a gracious lady who could sell fish hooks to trout, stuttered and stammered and finally got around to saying Char was just too New York for her position.

"Too New York? I haven't lived in New York in years! Some of the nicest people I know are from New York. How'd you like me to say all Southerners are lazy? Regional stereotypes aren't just offensive, they're unwarranted in today's mobile society—"

Char came to a grinding halt. Her boss was looking at her in mute despair, her expression saying better than words, "There, you see? I rest my case."

Too New York.

Char collected her pay and went home and cut off all her fingernails.

An hour later she considered her firing her first positive omen in months: without it she would have missed Ginger's call. Ginger, a Rockwood employee for more than twenty years, had remembered Char from her visits to the Rockwood estate during her boss's brief marriage to Beth Stiles. Ginger had a soft spot for Beth, and Char had no illusions that that was the main reason she had agreed to let her know if Harlan did anything unusual. It wouldn't exactly be spying, Char had explained; she would just be helping out an old friend of Beth's and letting her know what she'd only find out sooner or later. She had also confessed that she wasn't beyond resorting to the less-than-honorable tactics to keep an eye on Harlan, such as binoculars and camping out on estate property and interrogating the stable hands. *Real* spying.

Char had made a point of bringing Ginger postcards of Mill Brook Post & Beam. Picturesque though it was, it was still a sawmill, and Ginger didn't think a woman had any business working in such a place. "Well," Char had said, "Beth entrusted her entire savings with me. I guess she never thought Harlan would stoop to swindling her, no matter what had gone on between them."

Ginger had been persuaded, if with reservations. She believed Harlan was innocent. He was an honest man, she would tell Char. He couldn't survive in breeding and racing Thoroughbreds if he went around swindling people, especially his ex-wife and her best friend. In the end Ginger had agreed to spy for Char out of her firm belief in her boss's honesty.

Char didn't care about her motives: she just wanted to keep tabs on Rockwood. When she'd gotten her telephone on Tuesday—to keep her own ex-husband off her back about not being able to reach Em—Char had given Ginger the number.

That made two people who knew where to find her: Em's father and Ginger. Still, when the phone rang, Char's first thought wasn't either of them, but Adam Stiles. *He found my number... he's here in Nashville.*

She could have kicked herself for such soppy thinking. Whatever had happened between her and Adam over the weekend was finished. Adam probably considered it a nightmare by now. Even if he didn't he no doubt wished he did. Char hadn't heard a word from him all week. No note, no flowers, nothing. Not that she had contacted him, but how could she with Beth around Millbrook all the time?

Groaning, she warned herself to quit thinking about Adam. She'd just have to deal with him later. Right now she'd answer the damn phone. Probably some telemarketer, anyway.

"Miss Bradford?"

"Ginger! What a nice surprise. How are you?"

"Well ... I only wanted to tell you that Mr. Rockwood came home last night."

The rat. "Did he?"

"Yes, but he left again this morning."

"Oh?"

Ginger hesitated, and Char felt sympathy for the older woman, who obviously prided herself on her discretion. Char squelched the temptation to push, but she only felt a twinge of guilt: Harlan Rockwood had made his own bed and now he could lie in it.

Finally Ginger said, "He's gone to Vermont."

"Vermont—*oh no!*"

Before Ginger could hang up, Char capitalized on the housekeeper's sense of politeness and interrogated her with a series of rapid questions. Why Vermont? Where in Vermont? When would he be back? Did he mention Char or Beth? Did he know Char was still in Tennessee?

Ginger said she didn't know anything, except he was driving. "I believe Mr. Rockwood's very confused. He's an honest man."

Understanding she couldn't expect Ginger to have any other opinion, Char thanked her profusely, promised she wouldn't do anything rash and hung up.

Vermont.

That didn't bode well for keeping Beth out of the mess Char had made out of her life, with help, of course, from Harlan Rockwood. His unscrupulous actions were one thing. Char's own mistakes were quite another, and for those she would have to have a reckoning with herself at some point.

What was Rockwood doing in Vermont?

Char's heart lurched. Adam—

No, he wouldn't meddle. He had promised he wouldn't. Adam was a man of his word. *I could call him and ask him to keep an eye out for Harlan.*

"Uh-uh."

In for a penny, in for a pound. This disaster was her responsibility. Adam would help her if she asked; there was no question of that. He would have even before they had made love. That was the kind of man he was.

It wasn't, however, the kind of woman Char was: she couldn't let herself need Adam. If she had come to no other understanding with herself since his departure Sunday night, she had realized that she couldn't allow herself to be attracted to him out of a sense of her own desperation. If she was going to fall in love with Adam Stiles, it had to be because of who and what he was— not because she was afraid and alone and desperate.

She pushed him out of her thoughts, or at least into the back of her mind. She couldn't push him completely out. She knew that, because she'd tried.

It was foliage season in New England. Rich do-nothing that Harlan Rockwood was, he had probably headed to Vermont to see the pretty leaves.

Somehow, though, that didn't sound like him.

By the time Emily got home from school, Char was packed up and ready to go. "You're taking tomorrow off," she told her daughter, "and probably Monday, as well. I hate your missing school when you're not sick, but this is an emergency. We've got business up in Vermont."

Emily jumped up and down and hugged her mother, and jumped up and down some more, yelling, "We're going home!"

Char's heart sank as she forgot about Harlan and swindles and even Adam Stiles, confronted now, for the first time, with the raw reality of just how much Em missed Millbrook.

"Yeah, kiddo," Char said, her throat tightening with fear, anticipation, nostalgia . . . and sadness, she supposed, for the life she and her daughter had had in Vermont. Char had given it up not just for herself, but for her daughter, as well. Leaving had been Char's choice—

not a necessity, but a choice—and Emily had had little part in that decision.

She stroked Em's hair and held back the tears. "We're going home."

A SERIES OF MEETINGS kept Adam reasonably distracted on Friday morning, but by midafternoon he was brooding again. He had given up any lingering hope that time would make being away from Char easier. It didn't. As the days passed, he only grew more anxious to find out what she was up to. How was her new job, whatever it was? How was her food situation holding up? Had she come up with a plan for settling her dispute with Harlan Rockwood?

Did she ever think about coming home to Vermont?

Did she get lonely at night?

Did she regret the times they had made love?

His questions accentuated how far removed he was from her day-to-day life. He was a part of her past. He was a part of the life she had abandoned. A part of Millbrook.

He wasn't a part of her dreams. Was that what she was thinking now?

They were still unsettling questions. Questions he couldn't answer.

Questions, he thought, that made the weekend ahead seem interminable. He couldn't go back to Tennessee. He needed to stick around Millbrook for a weekend, not just for his kids' sake, but for his own. He had things to do around the house, errands to run, a life to live. Millbrook was home, and chasing a crackpot lawyer who hated it couldn't be all that smart.

But smart had damn little to do with his decision to stay home, and he knew it. He cared too much about

Char to put pressure on her by chasing her. For the first time in her life she was vulnerable: she had lost her great-aunt, her job, her home, her money. For years she had been known as one of Millbrook's sharpest, shrewdest citizens, and the prospect of coming home broke and swindled didn't sit well with her.

Who the hell was he kidding? The prospect of coming home at all didn't sit well with Charity Bradford. She was where she wanted to be.

Nevertheless, Adam felt that what was going on between them was real and lasting and would have happened if she had stayed in Millbrook or gone to Arizona to raise tarantulas or Saudi Arabia to raise camels or any other damn place to raise any other damn animal. It didn't matter that it was Tennessee and horses. It only mattered that he had finally woken up and discovered this captivating woman.

That didn't mean Char saw their relationship in the same light. She could have concluded that what had attracted him to her wasn't all he knew about her from having been around her a lifetime—her strength of character, her wit, her energy, her courage, her ability. Given her knack for putting words in his mouth and thoughts in his head, she could have concluded that what had attracted him to her was her present sorry state, that current, temporary vulnerability that had her broke and living in a tent just two weeks ago.

In which case he would have to straighten her out.

But even more worrisome, and less easily rectified, was if Char felt that her own sense of vulnerability was what had spurred *her* toward *him*. Adam hoped it wasn't so; he didn't believe it was. But he realized that if Char believed she had fallen for him out of her own sense of personal failure—out of fear and depression—they were in deep trouble. Ultimately she would end up resenting him for the very strength that had drawn her to him.

Other men might not mind feeding on a person's—especially a woman's—feelings of vulnerability and desperation, but Adam did mind. Being there for a lover was one thing. Absorbing her was quite another, and something he refused to do. Playing on Char's weaknesses had no appeal to him; that wouldn't make him feel stronger. When he had been vulnerable after Mel's death and his own disabling accident, Char hadn't played on his weaknesses. She had stood back and let him get his life back in order. They hadn't been lovers then, of course, maybe not even friends, but they had respected each other.

He hoped they still did.

He wanted Char to get back on her feet. If she needed his or anyone else's help, let her asking for it be a sign of strength and hope rather than of despair.

Adam groaned and slammed down his pen. He had analyzed all the reasons he couldn't go to Tennessee a thousand times since Monday. The bottom line was, the ball was in Char's court. It was her move. He was just going to have to grit his teeth and sweat it out.

"Excuse me—Adam?"

The voice was rich and deep, male, with the easy rhythm of the mid-South. Adam swung around and took in the tall, rangy figure, the piercing blue eyes, the tawny hair, and climbed to his feet, not bothering to hide his surprise. "You're the last person I expected to walk in here."

He and Harlan Rockwood shook hands. "Thanks for not throwing me out," the Tennesseean said dryly. "I know I'm likely to be boiled in oil around here."

Adam grinned. "Not with all the saws we have. Have a seat."

"Thanks, but I think I'll stay mobile."

"I don't blame you. She's not here..."

"I know. I checked for her car."

The infamous 1965 Chevrolet Bel Air driven by one Beth Stiles, former wife of Harlan Rockwood, a hardheaded woman who had long promised to run her ex-husband through the nearest saw should he show his face around Millbrook. Slow to anger and generally good-natured, Beth was known to hold a grudge once someone got on her bad side. With anyone but Harlan Rockwood, Adam would have wondered how he would have known her car. But he recalled his sister's tales of driving her bomb of a vehicle among the Rockwoods' sleek sports cars. They hadn't, to put it mildly, approved of her stubborn attachment to a car that had been old and battered even then.

"Will she be back soon?" Harlan asked.

"I'm not sure. You want to tell me why you're here?"

"Desperation," Harlan said with a deep sigh, sinking into the leather chair by his ex-brother-in-law's desk. "You heard Char Bradford bought into a Thoroughbred I own?"

Adam quickly decided to maintain an air of neutrality, if not outright ignorance, on the subject of Charity Bradford's business dealings. He said carefully, "I heard."

"I'll spare you the details, but things didn't work out. The horse didn't perform as expected and I had to pull him. It was a major disappointment for me—and for Char, as well, I'm sure."

An understatement to say the least, Adam thought. He sat at his desk and kept his eyes on Harlan Rockwood, unable to figure out what the man was up to. Why come to him? Had he seen him with Char in Nashville?

One thing was certain, Harlan Rockwood didn't look like a swindler.

The wealthy Tennesseean went on his always well-bred way, "The horse's decline was incredibly sudden and quite unpredicted. Well, one thing led to another, and I decided I had better investigate further." He leaned back in the chair and sighed heavily, looking tired and older than the boy who had swept Beth Stiles off her feet more than a decade ago. "Again, I'll spare you the details. Suffice to say, the horse I sidelined isn't the same horse I started racing a year ago."

Adam narrowed his eyes, just barely hanging on to his neutrality. "What are you saying?"

Harlan clenched his fists at his side, for him a major display of emotion. "I'm saying the horse I have in my pasture and have lost a considerable sum on is a ringer for the horse in which Char bought a share. My horse was stolen, apparently switched with this inferior one." The clear, deep blue eyes that fastened on Adam were enough to tell him of Harlan Rockwood's incisiveness—and his anger. For all his Southern charm and aristocratic breeding, this wasn't a man Adam would want to cross. His sister, of course, wouldn't think twice about it. Harlan added, "I came here in an effort to figure out what the hell's going on."

Adam paused, digesting this new information—or this new twist on old information. He wasn't sure which. "Then you're saying," he began judiciously, "that you didn't swindle Char?"

Harlan nearly choked. "Good Lord, of course I didn't swindle her! If anyone's been swindled, it's me. I've lost a fortune, not to mention a terrific horse."

"Have you called the police?"

"That was my first inclination, to be honest.'

Adam nodded, having a fair idea of what was coming next. "But you didn't."

"No."

"Instead you came to Vermont."

Harlan hesitated. "Yes. I—" He sighed, looking awkward, a rarity for him. "This is tricky."

It sure as hell was, Adam thought. "You remembered that Char and Beth are friends."

"Well, I've never had anything like this happen to me before."

"So, in retrospect, Char's popping up all at once and investing in this particular horse looks pretty damn suspicious."

Harlan merely shrugged, saying nothing.

"Do you think Char switched horses on you?" Adam asked.

"I don't know what to think, frankly. Look, Adam, I'm trying very hard not to jump to conclusions, but…" He paused, but Adam didn't miss the flash of pain in his face. Looking away, he said, "I don't know what Beth thinks of me. For all I know this is some elaborate scheme to get back at me for the misery I caused her."

"That would be criminal."

"Maybe things got out of hand and she and Char got in over their heads. They had to have help to pull off something like this. The horse business is crawling with unscrupulous people. It's difficult to know who to trust, particularly for a newcomer."

Which, Adam thought, was no doubt why Char had chosen to go into business with Harlan in the first place. Whatever his and Beth's problems had been, none had indicated Harlan Rockwood was anything but a wealthy, honest, intelligent Southern gentleman.

"Maybe you should talk to Char," Adam said. If she *had* swindled Harlan, she was going to unbelievable lengths to cover her tracks. Char did have a labyrinthine mind, but such deceit on her part seemed unlikely.

"That's why I'm here. I went by her office, but I gather she's moved to another location since returning to Vermont."

"What do you mean? Harlan, Char isn't in Vermont. She stayed in Tennessee."

Harlan's surprise seemed genuine. "I had no idea. Where's she living? When I'd thought we'd gotten into a bum deal together, I realized she'd lost more than she could afford to lose. She was trying to ride it out—she's as stubborn about that sort of thing as Beth—but obviously getting deeper into debt. There was nothing I could do about the horse and, well, she blamed me, naturally. I understood at the time, but I didn't want to be responsible for her losing even more than she already had. So I had her evicted from the house she was renting from me. The rent was fairly high," he said, adding dryly, "not that she was paying it."

Even if she had had the money, Adam knew, Char wouldn't have given Harlan another cent. "What a hellish mess," he said under his breath.

"I assumed she came back home and resumed her practice," Harlan said.

"Not a chance."

"Then what is she doing in Tennessee?"

"Regrouping. She lost a lot on that horse deal, Harlan."

"How much?"

Adam sighed, his instincts telling him not to meddle, his sense of honor telling him he had damn little choice. "Everything she had, just about."

Harlan paled. "I had no idea."

"Look, you and Char need to talk. I really don't want to get in the middle here."

"I understand, but, Adam, I need a handle on what's going on. Please . . ."

Before Adam could give into his all-too-human urge to blab everything, he heard the familiar roar of Beth's old Chevy outside. It needed a new muffler. If nothing else would get his sister to give up her bomb, it would be her contribution to acid rain and other air pollution problems.

Harlan recognized the distinct sounds of a Chevrolet of another generation and jumped to his feet. Adam noted with interest, and surprise, the jumble of emotions that crossed the man's face: fear, anger, excitement, reluctance, hurt. Mostly hurt, he decided. And swore silently. Adam now realized what before he only had suspected.

The poor bastard hadn't gotten over having lost Beth.

Whether the breakup of their marriage had been more her fault or Harlan's, Adam never knew and didn't care. It didn't matter. What had happened between them still pained his sister, although she would never admit as much. Now he knew it also pained his ex-brother-in-law.

"You can slip out the lower level," Adam said, pointing to the stairs.

Harlan didn't move. His eyes were locked on the front entrance.

"You'd better hurry," Adam said gently.

"Of course."

He disappeared within seconds of Beth bursting through the door, all hair and flailing arms and leather portfolio. "I know he's here," she yelled. "Tennessee license plate, fancy car. Where is the bum?"

"Beth—"

"Adam, if you cover for him, I swear I'll—"

"He was here. He just left through the lower level. If he's smart, he's moving fast."

Beth didn't listen further. She bounded back to the front door, tore it open and leaped outside. "Coward!" she yelled, and slammed the door, breathing hard.

"Missed him?" Adam asked mildly.

She gave her older brother a sheepish grin. "Didn't you hear the screech? Hope he doesn't take the signpost with him."

"Well, you can hardly blame the guy."

"I'd have been civilized," she said airily, but hoarsely, and she had to cough to get her voice back after so much yelling.

"Right."

"You want to tell me what's going on? First Char's spotted in town, now Harlan—"

Adam went rigid. "Char?"

"Yeah. As in Charity Winnifred Bradford. Hank spotted her car in the village. Adam, you okay? I doubt Char's after your hide unless—what'd you do to her in Tennessee?"

Ignoring his sister's probing look, Adam grabbed his jacket off the back of his chair. "Damned if I know what's going on," he told Beth. "But it's time I found out."

"I'm going with you."

"No." He had to think on his feet: "Look, I need you to cover for me with a client in twenty minutes. The file's right there on my desk."

"Adam—"

"Beth, please. I'll give you a full report."

"When?"

He shrugged. "I don't know."

"I don't like this, Adam," his sister said.

Adam didn't respond. Whatever her reasons, Char was in Vermont. In *Millbrook*.

She was home.

It wasn't much, but it was more than he'd had an hour ago. "I guess I'll get back when I get back."

"You do that," Beth said, and plunked herself down at his desk to look for his mythical file.

Adam got out of there in a hurry.

9

MILLBROOK HADN'T CHANGED in the year she had been gone.

As she and Emily walked down Main Street sipping lemonade, Char realized she had thought maybe it would. She should have known better, of course. But somehow she had anticipated—expected or hoped were too strong—that her absence would have had a visible effect on the community where she had grown up and spent the last five years of her adulthood.

How silly.

The air was crisp and bright, the autumn leaves at peak color, the scene worthy of a Vermont postcard.

It felt good to be back, Char decided. Not great, given the circumstances, but good. Better, certainly, than she had expected.

Emily darted into the open doorway of the bookshop and said hello to Ron, the proprietor, and patted Frost, Ron's overweight, lazy Siberian husky who had been a fixture on Main Street for years. Nowadays he mostly napped. Ron came out and greeted Char, asked how she was doing; she said fine and left it at that.

"We miss you around here," he said. "I do, for sure." He grinned that easy, low-key grin that had helped him earn the loyalty of so many customers. "I used to sell you a lot of expensive hardcovers."

"Those were the days," Char said, more cheerfully than she would have expected.

She dragged Emily away from Frost and continued along Main Street, moving inexorably along the same route she had taken countless times in the past.

That's right, she told herself, *the past. Not the present and not the future.*

The Nathan Stiles House on the south end of Main Street was still standing. The understated sign outside, the manicured lawn and flower beds, the sparkling paned windows, the white clapboards and black shutters, the slate-blue front door—everything was the same.

Except, of course, Charity W. Bradford was no longer listed among the professionals who occupied offices in the converted historical Colonial house. It had been built in the early nineteenth century by the first Stiles who had made his fortune as a sawyer on Mill Brook. The Stiles family had dispersed up along the river and around Millbrook Common, away from the village and the relative crush of Main Street. Char had never given much thought to working in the former drawing room where Adam's ancestors had lived and loved and died.

She tried not to now as she followed Emily into the entryway. The floor was gleaming cherry, the walls a subdued cream, the carpet on the graceful staircase a shade lighter slate-blue than the front door. Off to the left was where Char's office used to be.

"Look, Mom," Emily squealed, "nobody's there!"

Her old office was for rent, the accountant who had taken over her space apparently having departed. Char tried not to consider this development an omen, just something that was. She had simply given into human curiosity and come by to check out the place where she had spent so much time. So what if it were for rent?

"Can I go up and see Maria?" Emily asked, referring to the psychologist on the second floor.

Char said yes, then felt herself sagging as she watched her daughter bound up the stairs. So much energy. The entire trip north she had talked about seeing this person or that, stopping in this store or that. As far as Emily Bradford Williams was concerned, Millbrook couldn't be equalled. Char wondered if she had felt that way at seven. She couldn't remember.

Adam probably does, she thought.

"No."

She wasn't going to think about Adam Stiles. She wasn't here about the president of Mill Brook Post & Beam . . . about romance and passion and all *that*. She was here about Harlan Rockwood and thievery and getting herself out of one mess before she started getting into another.

She peered into the vacant rooms, remembering the Persian rug Aunt Mil had insisted on giving her, the big old Shaker table she had used as a desk, the tons of books and files and the computer that had seemed so incongruous amid the nineteenth-century lines of the former drawing room. The late-afternoon sun streamed in through the tall paned windows, making the two rooms seem even emptier and lonelier, reminding Char of exactly what she had given up for a dream.

For a dead dream.

"Looks pretty empty, doesn't it?"

Char whirled around just as Adam Stiles came through the double front door into the entryway. Her heart began to pound. He studied her, not coming too close. The uncompromising expression, the changeable eyes, the hardened muscles, the work shirt, the jeans, the boots—every inch of him looked a part of the

Vermont landscape. Even the gleaming hook where his left hand had been prompted images of men and women who lived lives of danger and hard work, who had carved livings out of the unforgiving mountains of northern New England for generations. Adam was a part of that tradition. So was Char. The difference was, it was a tradition he had no desire to escape, where she did—and had.

She managed a smile and said easily enough, "Fancy meeting you here." Trite, but it provided a few needed seconds to compose herself. She had been in a car for two days and looked it: her hair was all over the place, she had on no makeup and her jeans and sweatshirt had seen her through law school. "Guess I should have known better than to think I could be an anonymous presence in Millbrook for even an hour. You aren't here by accident, I take it?"

"Your car was spotted in town," he said, seldom one to mince words. "I heard about it."

"Figures. I've been in town an hour and already word's gotten upriver."

Adam shrugged. "Everybody knows what kind of car you drive. It was good for business, you know."

"What, driving a beat-up wreck?"

His eyes seemed to sparkle, and Char found herself remembering things she had no business remembering, at least not right now. First things first, she told herself.

"That's right," he said. "If you'd driven a big, fancy car, people around here would have wondered if you were looking after your interests disproportionately to looking after theirs."

Char knew what he was talking about. It wasn't a question of lawyer bashing, but one of balance. Earn-ing a comfortable living was one thing, something her clients understood and believed in. She did, after all, provide a necessary service and had the education, experience and expertise to do so. But living extravagantly, and rubbing people's noses in it, was quite another, particularly in a small town.

"Guess I'm living proof that not all lawyers are rich," she said. "How did you know I'd be here?"

"Even you couldn't resist a look at your old office."

"I just happened by."

"You're human, Char." He nodded toward her empty former office. "Any regrets?"

She shook her head. "Regret isn't the right word. It's more like nostalgia, maybe, except I'm not sentimental. What's Stan asking for rent these days?"

"Too much."

"You'd say that no matter how much he was asking."

"He told me he'd love to have you back. Said you could probably afford twice what he asked."

"Not anymore."

"Keep your nose out of the horse business, you never know," Adam said without condemnation or approval, just, as he would no doubt say, stating the facts. Before Char had a chance to get after him, he looked around and asked, "Where's Emily?"

"Upstairs visiting Maria."

"Avoiding her yourself?"

Char didn't squirm, but came close. She said innocently, "Why would I do that?"

"In case she started analyzing your reasons for going to Tennessee and losing all your money on a horse."

More "stating the facts," Char assumed, bristling. "Maria's always told me she doesn't analyze anyone who doesn't pay."

Adam grinned. "Think she'd be able to resist this one?"

"Probably not," Char said, laughing. "I wouldn't be surprised if she's pumping Emily for information, trying to find out if I'm certifiable or not."

Shifting his balance from one leg to the other, Adam gave Char a long look. She could feel her skin turning hot, could feel herself wanting to touch him, to be touched. He asked softly, "You going to tell me why you're in Vermont?"

"I guess I'd rather not go into it."

His eyes narrowed, and she could sense him pulling back from her, becoming distant and unapproachable. "I see."

"Because of Emily," Char added quickly. "It'll take time to explain and she'll be right down."

"I can assume, can't I, that you and Harlan Rockwood showing up in Millbrook on the same day isn't a coincidence?"

There was no amusement in his voice, but it was Char's turn to stand still and look distant, to conceal the emotions raging inside her. "You've seen him?" she asked coolly.

"He came by the mill. He—" Adam stopped when he heard a child's clambering footsteps on the staircase. He looked at Char. "We'll talk over dinner. I assume you haven't figured out where you're staying."

"I'm not worried about it."

"The hotels and inns are booked solid for peak weekend, even if you had considered spending money for a room, which I doubt. You didn't bring your tent, did you? We're expecting a frost tonight."

"No tent," Char said, tight-lipped. "But I can take care of myself. And Emily."

"Did I say you couldn't? If you're after Harlan, you won't want to stay with Beth—correct?"

She folded her arms across her chest, wondering just what Adam was getting at. His meddling always had a purpose. She said stiffly, "Correct."

Adam shrugged. "That leaves me."

"Look—"

"Dinner's at six-thirty. I'll put fresh sheets on in the guest room."

"Adam, the entire state of Vermont will know I'm staying with you."

He arched a brow at her. "So?"

So, indeed. Before she could think of a comeback, Emily burst in between them, yelling, "Uncle Adam!" He scooped her up, asking what her favorite food was, because whatever it was, that was what she was having for supper. So spaghetti and butterscotch pudding it was.

He put her down and grinned over the top of her head at Char. "Remember where I live?"

There was no graceful way out—exactly what Adam had planned, Char felt certain. He was trying hard not to look cocky and victorious. Char sighed. As if Harlan Rockwood, Millbrook, unemployment, debts and shattered dreams weren't enough for her to deal with. Now she had Adam Stiles, as well.

But wasn't that what she wanted?

She left the question hanging and told him, "Yeah, I remember."

IF ASKED A MONTH AGO, Char would have said she had been to Adam's house countless times. But as she pulled up his winding driveway, shaded by natural-growing hemlock and oak, she realized it couldn't have been more than a half-dozen times. Maybe not even that many. A big, airy, post-and-beam house constructed with Stiles lumber and sweat, it was nestled into the hillside above Mill Brook on fifty wooded acres. There were neighbors within walking, if not shouting, distance, so it wasn't as isolated as his brother Julian's place miles out on a dirt road. And it was close to the mill. With Adam that counted. Since Mel's death, however, his guests were more likely to be family members or the under-fourteen friends of his two preteen children, not people peripheral to his life.

As Char herself had been when she had lived in Millbrook.

In fact, most of her visits to Adam's house had occurred when Mel was still alive. Mel had hated moving out of town, but had never said so, instead pretending that what she wanted was anything Adam wanted. If he preferred a quiet life in the woods above the river that had made his family's living for generations, then so did she. Except, of course, that meant she was living a lie—and such lies weren't easily kept secret. Adam had known. Everyone in Millbrook had known that Mel Stiles was an unhappy woman.

Char parked behind Adam's pickup and leaned back for a moment, enjoying the cool late-afternoon breeze through her open window. She couldn't have played the martyr the way Mel had. She was no good at suffering in silence and even less adept in pretending. Keeping her clients' confidences, yes. She could be closemouthed when she needed to be. But not speaking her mind, especially when someone had sought out her opinion? Never. Adam had consulted Mel about building a house out of town, but instead of telling him how she felt, she had said, in effect, "Whatever you want, honey."

Mel had been a lively, interesting woman who had adored Adam and their two children. If only she had been less confused about what and who she should be. "Just be yourself," Beth, who had reported her comments back to Char, used to tell her sister-in-law. "It's all anyone can ask you to be. Nothing more, nothing less."

On that particular score Char had never had a problem. It was in the areas of compromise and opening herself up to other people—allowing them into her life, allowing herself the occasional mistake—where she sometimes tripped up.

Or fell flat on her face, as the case may be, she thought dismally.

She exhaled, aware of Emily staring at her in curiosity, but she wasn't ready to move yet. She could hear the river tumbling over the rocks down by the road on its way from the mountains to join with the Connecticut River, then on with it into Long Island Sound. It had been Adam who had explained Mill Brook's microrole in the earth's ecology, back when she was nine or ten and had complained that it wasn't much of a river. Big rivers are made up of little rivers, he had told her.

Strange, she thought, that she only just now was remembering that episode with Beth's older brother. Before Nashville she would have said it had never happened, that Adam had almost never talked to her. Given their age difference, more pronounced in childhood, she supposed he must have seemed more remote to her growing up than he actually had been.

Mill Brook was, in fact, a beautiful river—a creek, the folks in her adopted state would call it. Char had come to recognize, if not appreciate, its picturesque quality even before she had left the town of Millbrook for the first time after her high school graduation. It was then that she had made her now-infamous remark about how much beauty a person could stand.

And Tennessee certainly was a beautiful state. Harlan Rockwood's place along the Cumberland River rivaled any in Vermont—or anywhere else, for that matter.

So why had the bastard swindled her? It wasn't as if he needed the money.

"Mom, aren't we going in?"

Char looked at her daughter and smiled. "Nothing like an impatient child to rouse a mother from thinking things she's got no business thinking in the first place." She looked at Adam's natural-stained house and sighed. "As I'm always telling you, Em, first things first."

Harlan she would have to deal with later. Right now she had to concentrate her energies on getting through the evening—*the night*—with Adam Stiles. At least they would have three children in the house. As much as Char wanted to work out their relationship, or whatever it was they had, she had other things she needed to work out first.

Dinner.

Then bed alone or with, at most, Emily.

Then Harlan Rockwood in the morning.

That was her plan, and she would just have to stick to it. She didn't need complications right now.

Was that what Adam was—a complication?

She remembered their afternoon together, and suddenly the breeze off the river wasn't nearly cool enough.

"*Mom*," Emily groaned impatiently.

"Okay, okay. Let's go."

The air, crisp and icy clear, smelled of autumn and the woods. Oddly, Char felt herself begin to relax as she joined Emily on the flagstone walk to the side entrance. Adam's was the sort of front door used only by salesmen and bill collectors. Tucked into the hillside as it was, the house had only a small yard, the land cleared enough for vegetable and flower gardens and a patch of grass where two ancient Adirondack chairs sat in the shade of a sugar maple, its leaves a vibrant orange. In the woods along the perimeter of the yard, Char noticed various knotted ropes and tire swings dangling from trees.

So did Emily. "Oooh," she said. "Think Abby and David'll want to swing?"

"It'll be dark soon," Char pointed out, trying not to picture her daughter swinging like Tarzan over the hillside. The Stiles family had always had a fatalistic attitude toward broken limbs and skinned knees. Char could remember the antics she and Beth had performed on various rocks and trees when they were children. She had hoped her daughter would be more sensible.

Children, her Aunt Mil would have said, will be children.

Adam was waiting for them just inside the door, his hook discarded, his expression filled with warmth and satisfaction as he gave Em a hug and tousled her hair. With his children standing behind him, he didn't touch Char, just said, "Hello. Glad you could come."

"Me, too," she mumbled, somewhat taken aback. The man was so damn outrageously sexy. *How* could she have not noticed before?

Abby and David couldn't wait to whisk Emily off to work a thousand-piece jigsaw puzzle they had just

started in the family room. Being reasonably man-
nerly children, however, they first greeted Char, welcoming her like a long-lost, somewhat wayward aunt
who'd finally returned to her senses and come home.
She might have spent the past year on the moon, never
mind just a thousand miles away in Tennessee.

"Did you really take Dad to Opryland?" Abby asked.
Except for her huge blue eyes, she was every inch her
father's daughter. "He said you talked him into going
on the Cannonball."

Char laughed. "I did."

"Did he scream?" David, younger and fairer, like his
mother, asked.

"Only a little. He even went on the Grizzly River
Rampage. Did he tell you he got soaked head to toe?"

And that afterward we made love? But Char knew
that Adam played his romantic cards very close to his
chest. His children wouldn't have an inkling of what
was going on between them until he was good and
ready to tell them. And when, she wondered, would
that be? When she tucked her tail between her legs and
ran home to Vermont?

Emily, still sore that her mother had gone to Opryland without her, didn't want to hear any more, so the
subject was quickly abandoned and the under-twelve
crowd vanished.

There was an awkward silence between the two
adults left standing in the entry.

"They're great kids," Char commented, just to say
something.

Adam leaned against the wall, looking even taller
than he had in Nashville, his eyes, dark in the shadows, on her. "They have their moments," he said,

straightening up suddenly. "Want to give me a hand in the kitchen?"

"Sure. There isn't a whole lot to fixing spaghetti and butterscotch pudding."

"True," he said as they entered his large oak kitchen. "Unless you'd prefer to eat with them in the family room and watch *Star Trek* on the VCR, we're having fresh lemon sole with salsa and new potatoes in the dining room."

"Adam, you didn't have to go to all that trouble."

"I know." He looked at her and smiled. "The last woman I had to dinner was my sister Beth. Let me enjoy myself."

"I should be buying you dinner," Char said, remembering everything Adam had already done for her—never mind that she hadn't asked him to do anything.

"You'll have your chance."

She nodded grudgingly. "I hate being insolvent."

"Insolvent? Is that lawyer talk?"

"It doesn't sound as harsh as broke, but it means the same thing."

"I know what it means," Adam said softly. He pulled out the salad bowl and set it on the kitchen table along with the spaghetti, pot of sauce and meatballs and Italian bread already there. "Just making sure—"

"That I'm looking reality square in the eye?" Char finished for him. "It's impossible not to in my situation, believe me. I wake up every night in a sweat wondering how I'm going to get through the next month. I used to have a five-year financial plan. Now—hell, now I'm just worried about getting food on the table and keeping a roof over our heads."

"Be glad you're young."

"I'm not looking for anyone to solve my problems for me, you know," she said abruptly.

Adam opened a bottle of salad dressing, sweetened with Vermont maple syrup, and set it beside the salad bowl. "Not waiting for a knight on a white horse to gallop up to your place and whisk you off into the sunset?"

Char laughed. "Honey, if I start seeing white horses and knights, somebody better lock me up."

"Probably won't come to that. I don't think any red-blooded knight would mistake you for a damsel in distress."

"I hope not."

"An intelligent, smart-mouthed, occasionally grouchy, sometimes captivating woman who's had her share of setbacks the past year or two, yes. But not a damsel in distress."

"*Sometimes* captivating?"

"Well," Adam said, grinning, "you're not all that captivating when you're sending me off on wild-goose chases or telling my kids tales about their father."

"You did scream—"

"*After* Opryland," Adam corrected, giving her a look that turned her insides to jelly. "Not during."

While she tried to think of an appropriate comeback, Adam called Abby, David and Emily to dinner. No waiter, he showed the three children the plates, the silverware wrapped in napkins and the food lined up on the table. They were to load up their plates and scat.

"There will be no dessert," he instructed, "until the salad's gone—and remember Jasper isn't fond of lettuce." Jasper was their golden lab, a big, overly friendly animal who was relegated to the back rooms of the sprawling post-and-beam house. "If you try to pawn off your salad on him and he gets sick, it's your responsibility."

Char assumed Adam had based his warning on precedent and she should keep her mouth shut about discussing a sick dog before dinner, just as Adam had refrained from comment when she and Emily had discussed dinner entrées in Nashville. Hot dogs versus steak, she recalled. It seemed so damn long ago.

Abby and David promised Jasper was off-limits. "I do, too," Emily said, "but do I have to eat the radishes?"

Adam glanced at Char for an answer, but Abby volunteered to eat Em's radishes if she could get out of eating red peppers, and they were off, trading vegetables, before the adults could butt in with their opinion.

"They must be healthy," Adam muttered. "They keep growing."

Their own dinner was a cinch to prepare, especially since Adam's version of salsa merely required opening a jar. The lemon sole, he explained, was day-boat, purchased at his favorite deli and fish market in Bennington. Abby and David liked fish, but not spicy salsa—but Adam liked spaghetti. He didn't, however, like butterscotch pudding: he and Char were splurging and having Kahlua cheesecake made by the Nuns of New Skete over the border in upstate New York.

"Pure decadence," Char said, uncorking the wine bottle.

"Maybe the fish'll counteract the cheesecake."

She shook her head. "Good never counteracts bad."

"Speaking of which," Adam said as he sprinkled the piping hot new potatoes with minced fresh parsley, "did you hook up with Harlan this afternoon?"

"That snake—no. I kept an eye out for him, but he knows my car. Probably knows I'm in town, too." She noticed something funny about Adam's expression. "You know something about that?"

"I don't want to get in the middle between you two..."

"You already are."

He scowled at her. "You can be merciless, you know."

"You're no saint yourself. Well?"

Adam sighed. "I told him you were in Tennessee. He wants to talk."

"Yeah, I'll bet! He probably found out I'd been camping on his property and now he wants to sue me for trespassing."

"You could give him a chance to explain himself."

Char shot Adam a look, narrowing her eyes. "You know something I don't know, don't you?"

He got the fish out of the oven and shook his head, pretending to be far more absorbed in his cooking than he had any right to be: about all there was left to do was switch off the broiler.

Char wasn't about to let him off the hook. "What did Harlan tell you when you saw him?"

"Nothing he won't tell you when you see him."

"But something I don't already know," she suggested.

"Look, Char, I'm not on the witness stand here. My conversation with Harlan was private—just as my conversations with you are. I didn't relate anything to him about your version of events, merely recommended that the two of you sit down and talk."

"Don't you think I've tried that? The bastard keeps avoiding me."

"Human instinct," Adam muttered dryly as Char stomped off into the dining room with the wine bottle.

"I heard that."

"You were supposed to."

"Are you siding with that man?"

"No," he said, standing in the doorway. "I'm not siding with anyone."

"You just want us to talk," she said, taken aback by her own scathing tone.

Adam shrugged. "If you were your own lawyer, Char, what would you counsel yourself to do?"

She scowled, hanging on to the cold neck of the wine bottle. "Talk to the swindler." Sighing, she looked at Adam and smiled. "I do get hot under the collar whenever his name comes up, don't I?"

"Better him than me," Adam said.

"Does Beth know he's in town?"

Adam cleared his throat and straightened. "Yes."

"Yipes."

"Yipes, indeed. Can you almost feel sorry for the poor bastard?"

"Almost," Char said, and poured the wine. "I'll have to tell Beth everything now, won't I?"

"I would before she drags it out of you."

"I just don't want her to feel responsible for what happened to me. If Harlan swindled me because I'm Beth's friend, then so be it. That's not her fault—it's his. And mine. I should have known better than to do business with him in the first place."

"You don't have to protect Beth," Adam said, heading back to the kitchen. "She doesn't approve of knights and white horses, either."

By silent, mutual agreement they abandoned the subjects of Harlan Rockwood and horses as they got dinner on the table. They could hear *Star Trek* music and the occasional whine about offensive vegetables from the family room, but Adam put on Vivaldi in the background, and it was almost as if he and Char were alone.

Adam raised his wineglass, the sharp angles of his face softened in the candlelight. "To quiet children."

Char laughed, seconded his toast and they clinked glasses. Their fingers brushed, and she could feel the tension in her spine begin to ease. Adam wasn't going to put her on the spot about Harlan or Millbrook—or even themselves. For tonight, at least, she could put everything on hold and just relax.

10

CHAR'S INSTINCTS were accurate as far as they went: Adam *didn't* put her on the spot during dinner. They restricted their conversation to nonthreatening topics, and Adam was amiable enough, if somewhat distant. He seemed to be holding back—information, his opinions, himself. Char wasn't sure what. She felt as if he had constructed an invisible wall around him that she couldn't penetrate. Whether deliberately or unconsciously, he had made himself—or at least a part of himself—unavailable to her. He wasn't withdrawn or unpleasant...just a little distant. And she realized, with some surprise, that she didn't want that.

So what did she want?

What she wanted, she had to admit, was to know what Adam Stiles was thinking, be it good or bad.

What she wanted was a full, honest relationship with him.

Commitment.

A life, she thought as she waited for him in the living room, its neutral tones helping to soothe her nerves. They had already done up the dishes and sent bowls of butterscotch pudding into the family room, where Abby, David and Emily were immersed in their movie and jigsaw puzzle. Adam was pouring after-dinner brandy.

Then off to the guest room with you and Em, Char thought, sighing. It was just as well. What she didn't need right now was another complication.

Was that what Adam was—a complication?

He came into the living room and handed her a brandy snifter, then went back for his and settled into the chair catty-corner from her seat on the couch. She noticed that: he hadn't joined her on the couch.

What are you thinking, Adam Stiles?

But since he wasn't putting her on the spot, she didn't want to put him on the spot. Fair play's turnabout, he could tell her.

Or, as it turned out, she could tell him.

"Do you hear a car?" she asked, sitting forward with her brandy.

Adam glanced at his watch. "It's seven-thirty already?"

"Why? Is someone supposed to be here at seven-thirty?" *Not Harlan*, she thought. *Please not Harlan. I don't want to deal with him right now—not in front of Adam, thank you.* She narrowed her eyes at him. "Adam, what's going on?"

"Julian and Holly are joining us for brandy."

Char had always gotten along with Adam's younger brother Julian, and she still laughed when she thought about how Holly Wingate Paynter, Texan by birth and Vermonter by heritage, had taken Millbrook—and Julian Stiles—by storm earlier that year. A storyteller by trade and by nature, Holly could still confuse her husband about when she was telling the truth and when she wasn't.

"Holly has several new children's stories she wants to try out," Adam said. He sounded so innocuous as he climbed to his feet. "So she asked if she could take

Abby, David and Emily back to their place. I should have mentioned it before now, but I just didn't get around to it."

"She couldn't try out her stories here?"

"Wouldn't work as well, I guess. Wrong atmosphere."

Adam's back was to Char, so she couldn't see his face to judge if he were stretching the truth. "And this was Holly's idea?"

"Julian's actually." Adam disappeared into the kitchen. "He knew she was itching for a tryout audience, and the light bulb went on when he found out I'd have three critics here tonight."

"Nice guy. Will the kids be up late? I could pick them up later."

"Oh, there's no need."

Char's heart began to pound. "Julian and Holly barely have enough room for themselves in that house, never mind three kids."

"Three spoiled kids, maybe. Sleeping bags in front of the fireplace sounds good to me."

It would sound good to Emily, too, after the variety of accommodations she had endured during the past year. Char leaned back and sipped her brandy, surprised at the rush of relief and warmth she felt. Adam Stiles had been plotting to get her alone, but she didn't feel pressured. Instead she felt wanted.

"You've got a generous brother and sister-in-law," she said.

Adam emerged from the kitchen with two empty glasses in his hand and the bottle of brandy tucked under his left arm. "After their antics last winter," he said, "my brother and sister-in-law owe me one."

JULIAN AND HOLLY stayed just long enough to drink a glass of brandy and not ask too many questions before whisking the three kids off. Adam told his brother he'd be by in the morning, but Julian wasn't worried. He had plenty to keep the kids busy, including making apple cider. Abby and David were excited about getting to hear one of Holly's new stories, and they always loved to spend the night at Uncle Julian and Aunt Holly's small post-and-beam house out in the woods. Emily was delighted to do whatever Abby and David were doing.

Char joined Adam in seeing them off, then returned inside, where she helped him get a fire going in the big granite fireplace in the living room. Neither spoke. Adam didn't mind. He knew Char had a lot on her mind and was willing to give her space. It was okay with him that they could be together and not have to fill every second with talk.

After the fire caught, Char flopped back onto the couch. Adam could tell something was on her mind, but he stayed in front of the fireplace, stirring the kindling with the poker.

"Word'll be around town by noon tomorrow that we're seeing each other," Char said finally.

Adam shrugged and glanced back at her. "Word's already around town."

"Terrific. I come here for dinner and the whole town's talking."

"Town's been talking a whole lot longer than just today. They've been at it ever since I headed down to Tennessee to find out what you were up to. Folks know I wouldn't do that just for a friend of Beth— I'd make her do it. According to town gossip, I had my own personal agenda." He stabbed at a red-hot chunk of birch. "Which is true."

"Well, I don't know where people get their ideas. I've always considered you a friend, too."

Adam arched his brow. "That right?"

"Well—"

"Well, nothing. You and I didn't have much good to say about each other until we ended up in the sack together. And even then."

Char sniffed. "I would hardly call what we did a grudge match."

"Neither would I," Adam said, sighing. How the hell was he going to get through to this woman without making her feel as if he had backed her into a corner? "Anyway, that's all just town talk. Mostly I ignore it."

"People should mind their own business."

"They should, but they don't."

He dropped onto his knees and leaned back against his heels so he could grab an oak log one-handed and toss it onto the fire. Then he poked at it, making sure its weight wouldn't smother the flames. All was well. He backed away from the fireplace and sat on the carpet with his back against the couch, inches from Char's knees.

She slid off the couch and sat next to him, her shirt riding up high on her stomach. She quickly pulled it down. "A fireplace isn't as efficient as a wood stove, you know," she said.

He smiled at her, aware of the scent of her light perfume, noticing the paleness of her skin. She had had a hard day, he would guess. Probably a hard couple of days. But far be it for Charity Bradford to whine to anyone about her troubles.

"A wood stove isn't as romantic," he pointed out.

"I never figured you for someone who would take romance over efficiency. Or was the fireplace Mel's idea?"

"No, it was mine," he said without awkwardness. Talking about Mel no longer bothered him. She was his children's mother and a lost friend, but the passion and grief he had once felt for her were past now, gone. "She left everything up to me—which I should have realized was her way of telling me she didn't want to move out here. I'm not good at reading between the lines, I guess. People have something to say to me, they'd better go on and say it."

Char kicked off her shoes and wiggled her toes, looking more relaxed than she had when Julian and Holly were here. Adam took that as a positive sign that she didn't feel strange and out-of-place in his company, in his house.

She grinned at him. "Are you saying you're thick-headed?"

He laughed. "Guess so." And he stretched his legs out next to hers, resisting the urge to rub his thigh up against hers. "So what did you do this afternoon since you didn't find Harlan and have it out with him?"

"I went out to Aunt Mil's place and had a look around. The new owners have already fixed it up a lot. They were very gracious to me and let me look around. They hope to open a bed-and-breakfast by next fall. Aunt Mil would have liked that, I think. She always said it was too much house for one person—her only regret about not having had children herself. She loved company."

"How do you feel about the changes?" Adam asked quietly, sensing the lingering grief Char felt whenever she talked about her great-aunt.

She shrugged. "Okay—better than I had expected. I wasn't sure at first I wanted to go out there, but Em kept bugging me. She wanted to see the old place. It was sad with Aunt Mil not there; Em cried a little. I think we both half expected we'd see Aunt Mil sitting in her porch swing or setting out mums, chasing a cat out of her herb garden. She really hated cats. I used to tell her that wasn't very spinsterish of her, and she'd just glare at me. Anyway, the porch swing's gone. The Eberharts are having it painted and repaired."

"It's nice that they didn't junk it."

"It is, although it's not a valuable antique or anything. Aunt Mil picked it up in the fifties at a flea market. She bought it specifically for the house, so I felt it was more a part of the place than of her, or I might have kept it."

"The Eberharts have done work in the yard, too, haven't they?" Adam asked, knowing they had. He hadn't been by the Bradford place in months, but he'd heard talk in town that it was finally getting spruced up. There were those who had valued Millicent Bradford as a teacher and town volunteer while complaining about her less-than-meticulous ways as a home owner. As far back as he could remember, people had tried to talk her into hiring a handyman. Even, if he believed town gossip, her grandniece Char had a go at the stubborn Yankee. Mil had rebuffed all comers, claiming she liked her place just the way she kept it.

"They pruned the hell out of the herb garden and rosebushes, which they needed, and took down the dead elm by the mailbox and did what they could about the blackberry bushes. It's a different place, really. But the same, too. The herbs and roses will come back, and they and the lilacs and most of the other trees and perennials were all planted by Aunt Mil or my great-grandparents."

Adam could hear the pain—the guilt—in Char's voice, but he didn't sense she was looking to him to change the subject. "What about the house itself?"

"Well, they're not painting it chartreuse or anything. They're insulating and putting in new windows, doing some rewiring and plumbing, but they're going to extraordinary lengths to preserve the 'architectural integrity'—their words—of the house itself. And they want to preserve its history, a sense of the personalities who built the house and lived in it for so many generations." Char looked at Adam, the flames of the fire blazing in her sad, stubborn eyes. "All Bradfords, of course."

Adam could guess what was on her mind. "You did what you felt you had to do when you sold the place."

"Did I?"

"That's something only you can answer," he said. Then, after a moment, he added, "Or have any right to ask. It's none of anyone else's business."

Char pulled her knees up under her chin and wrapped her arms around her ankles. "I could have hung on to the place, you know."

Adam said nothing.

"It would have taken most of my savings and everything Aunt Mil had left me to pay the taxes and even do the basic work on cleaning up and modernizing the house, but I could have managed."

"If you'd wanted a rambling old house and ten acres of land."

"Look what I got instead." But before he could comment, she added quickly, "Imagine what my ancestors went through to get that house and land."

"And why do you suppose they did? So future Bradfords would feel forced to live there? That's not what I want for my kids, and I doubt that's what they wanted for theirs. When I'm gone, this place'll be Abby and David's to keep or to sell—if I haven't gotten rid of it and moved to Florida by then."

Char shot him a look and grinned. "Not a chance."

"You never know. From what I recall, Char, Mil hesitated about leaving you the house in the first place. She wanted to spare you the guilt over having to decide what to do with it. I think she finally decided guilt's not your style." He looked at her, the firelight making her hair shine, her pale skin glisten. "It isn't, you know."

"Maybe not, but that doesn't mean..." She didn't finish, sighing as she kicked out her legs once more. "The fact is, I could have kept the house. Instead I sold it and virtually everything I own and gave up my law practice and invested my profits in a dud horse. So now I have nothing."

"Don't you?" Adam asked, and for the first time he thought he understood what had sent Charity Bradford to Tennessee a year ago. Not her dream—not her passion for her horses or her willingness to put everything in a deal with Harlan Rockwood. A dream was as personal and individual as anything Adam could imagine. But he thought he understood why, then, it had been now or never. He went on, "Imagine for a moment you did hang on to the Bradford house. Where would you be today?"

"I'd have a home," she said. "So would Emily."

"You'd be knee-deep in insulation, layers of wallpaper, mice skeletons, extension cords, dead bushes—and wondering what life would have been like if you had grabbed for the brass ring instead."

"I suppose. And what has this experience taught my daughter?"

"A little about what counts in life and what doesn't."

Char turned toward him, her hair falling in her eyes as she searched his face. "You're serious, aren't you?"

"Yes."

"You wouldn't have done what I did, but you don't condemn me?"

"I don't condemn you, Char," he said carefully. "That doesn't mean I don't think you're not crazy for living like a damn rat instead of calling on your friends for help. But that has to do with pride, not dreams."

She tilted her head back. "Sometimes you amaze me, Adam Stiles. And you're right. I made my choice a year ago and I was so excited. I've never had such a rush as when I packed up and headed to Tennessee. I did what I wanted to do and ended up broke."

"But not in debt," Adam pointed out cheerfully.

"Who'd lend a broke woman money?" She laughed suddenly, her eyes shining. "Any more brandy left?"

"Sure."

He climbed to his feet and divided the last of the bottle between their two glasses, handing Char hers before he sat back beside her.

She smiled and held her glass up for a toast. "To Aunt Mil—for making dreams possible, for me *and* for the Eberharts." She and Adam clinked glasses and drank up, and she settled back, getting cozy. "Strange how one person's nightmare can be another person's dream. Those people *love* that house."

"And Millbrook."

"What's there not to love about Millbrook?"

"Lots. We've both lived here long enough to know that." Adam knew they were moving into more intimate territory now, venturing closer to talking about them and what had gone on between them in Nashville. His eyes on her, Adam asked, "Has a new dream replaced the old one of getting out of Millbrook?"

"It wasn't just getting out of Millbrook," she explained. "It was also going to Tennessee and raising horses—a positive motivation, not just a negative one. And the timing seemed perfect. Aunt Mil was gone. I had a bunch of cases go sour on me all at once. I wanted out, and I got out."

"Have you ever looked back?"

"You know I have."

"But?"

"But I'm not willing to give up, Adam. Not yet. I've got to figure out what's going on with Harlan. Then I'll go on from there. I love Tennessee, and I love the idea of raising horses, if not the reality. I don't know. Right now when I think of where I want to live, it's in terms of a place with enough electrical outlets and a dishwasher."

"The advantages of new construction," Adam said.

"Said the president of Mill Brook Post & Beam."

Her smile nearly knocked him over with its brightness, its way of warning him that Charity Bradford may have blown her dream, but she wasn't a failure. She hadn't given up, and if coming home to Millbrook would mean she had, Adam didn't want any part of it. They would just have to work something out. At least, he thought, as far as he was concerned.

He touched her hair, feeling the softness of her cheek through it, and found her mouth, kissing her lightly. He felt so warm around her. So alive. Not just a father, a brother, a businessman, but simply, a man. The rest were roles he played, important roles; they contributed to who he was. But with Char, he didn't have to worry about the right response to her report card or the environmental consequences of logging a certain tract of land. He could just be himself. He could discuss those things with her, share his concerns with her—and his triumphs and joys.

Even if she stays in Tennessee?

"Yes," he breathed, his mouth finding hers again.

"What did you say?" she asked.

He smiled. "I said come to bed with me."

LOCATED IN A SEPARATE WING off the first floor, Adam's bedroom, with the strength and simplicity of its lines and decor, was a reflection of the man who lived there. A tall, paned window, almost as high as the cathedral ceiling, overlooked the back woods.

"Do you worry about bears climbing into bed with you at night?" she asked.

"Nope. I'm too restless. Being in the woods makes you nervous?"

She shook her head. "I have a feeling bears are the least of my worries."

"I don't know as I've never seen a bear out back here."

"Keep a shotgun in the closet just in case?"

"No guns around the kids. The risk of an accident's a lot greater than the risk of a bear. And you ought to know we don't have many bears around here—and none to worry about. This place isn't anywhere near as isolated as it might seem."

He was right, and she knew it. Char felt removed from the pressures of civilization, but not isolated: the main road into town was at the end of the driveway. Still, she was undeniably, if inexplicably, tense.

Pushing her uneasiness to the back of her mind, she observed that the handsome bedroom also had a separate entrance onto a terrace, and its own granite fireplace. Adam hunched over it, quickly and deftly starting a fire.

"Do you have a fire in here every night?" she asked. "When it's cold, I mean."

"No—only when the spirit moves me. Sometimes I'll build a fire and sit and read a book just to settle down after a long day. Usually I don't bother and just read near the fire in the family room."

"Then I'll feel honored."

He glanced over his shoulder at her, but didn't smile. "You should."

The uneasiness came over her again. She felt warm and jumpy, anxious—even self-conscious—if not exactly nervous.

She cleared her throat and rubbed her hands together, not reassured to notice her palms were clammy. "I'd like to get the road dust off me, if that's all right."

He kept his attention focused on the fire and just pointed without looking around at her. "Bathroom's down the hall, second door."

It was a functional, pleasant bathroom with an oversize white tub, a white pedestal sink and shelves piled with white Egyptian cotton towels. Char filled the tub with water as hot as she could stand and tossed in a capful of almond-scented bath and shower gel. The water bubbled as she peeled off her clothes.

You need to relax, Ms. Charity, she told herself.

If only she could pinpoint exactly what was wrong. Or maybe *wrong* wasn't the correct word. Not right, anyway. Something just wasn't right with her.

She wished she knew what Adam was thinking. That certainly had to be a factor in her unsettled mood. She could ask him, of course. They could talk, analyze, rationalize. What did he think about her? About himself? About *them?* It would all get very serious and no doubt one or the other would bring up horses and Tennessee and Harlan Rockwood.

She didn't want to talk, she realized. She didn't want to think too much.

Maybe that was the problem. What she wanted—and this just wasn't like her at all—was just to go with the moment. Be spontaneous. Act without an agenda. Just let happen whatever was going to happen.

Yet . . . she was a practical woman. And practical women didn't go around sleeping with old friends and generating small-town gossip unless there was, as Aunt Mil would say, some future in it.

Unless Adam loved her.

Unless she loved Adam.

She was taking risks with her reputation, her peace of mind, her lifelong friendship with the Stiles family by continuing whatever it was she was continuing with Adam. An affair? A brief, wild fling? They were much too sensible for that sort of thing . . . weren't they?

It was entirely possible, her rational side told her, that ultimately they could prove just to have needed each other at the same time. There was nothing tawdry or regrettable about needing someone, about being there for someone, especially a friend. And who cared what anyone else thought? Let the gossips gossip; she and Adam would explain the score to whomever needed to know. If what they had now, what they felt for each other, was based on little more than a coincidence—a fleeting need for love and passion when both were feeling particularly vulnerable—then so be it.

Except it didn't feel that way to her.

It felt like, if she were willing to be honest with herself, something lots more than coincidence and vulnerability.

It felt a whole lot more like love.

Char knew that sooner or later she and Adam were going to have to figure out what they meant to each other. She was going to have to push past his emotional remoteness—that damn Yankee reserve of his—and find out what he felt. Tell him what she felt.

But better later than sooner.

She slid into the steaming water and instantly felt the tension ease out of her muscles . . . and her mind. Tonight, at this moment, she and Adam were right for each other. She would deal with tomorrow when it came.

After a few minutes a knock on the door roused her from her temporary sense of peace. Adam asked, "May I come in?"

Hear heart began to pound. "Certainly."

He entered the bathroom, and something about his being fully dressed and her nakedness struck her as inordinately sexy. She could feel her nipples hardening, her entire body becoming tingly and excited. Both her earlier uneasiness and short-lived calm were distant memories now.

"Want some company?" he asked, sitting on the edge of the tub.

Char sank lower into the water under the inadequate cover of the bubbles. "Sure."

In the dim light it was impossible to tell what color his eyes were. He dipped his hand into the steamy water and pushed the bubbles down toward the end of the tub, exposing her breasts to his view. She thought he would touch her, but he didn't. He reached toward her knees and scooped up a handful of bubbles and, grinning, put them on her chin.

"You could never pass for Santa Claus," he said.

"Watch it before I pull you in here with me, clothes and all."

"Takes too long to get out of wet clothes, especially one-handed."

She laughed. "Then maybe I won't pull you in, after all."

He gently pushed the bubbles off her chin, smoothing them down her neck, his fingertips barely skimming the surface of her skin. Every millimeter of her was sensitized to him as the warm, silky water swirled around her.

"Sweet torture, isn't it?" he murmured.

"For me or for you?"

"Both of us."

His fingers shot under the bubbles and flicked against her breasts before he pulled his hand from the water. "Can't stay at that for long without going crazy," he muttered. "Every day since I left Tennessee I've imagined you here like this. The reality, I assure you, is far more irresistible than the fantasy."

She smiled at him. "Who wants you to resist?"

He laughed and stood up, pulling his shirt out of his jeans. He unbuttoned it slowly and deftly with his one hand. Char watched, transfixed. He hung the shirt on a hook on the door and pulled his undershirt over his head, Char unabashedly taking in the sight of his hard abdomen and chest.

He caught her staring and dipped his hand into the tub, flicking bubbles onto her cheek. "Voyeur," he said, laughing.

"What am I supposed to do, go underwater and hold my breath until you're finished?"

"Watch all you want."

She did, and when he was naked, she could see that her watching had had its effect on him, as well. He climbed into the tub with her, their legs tangling and water splashing over the sides.

"I don't think we're going to last in here very long," Char said, her mouth dry with anticipation.

"Agreed," he replied. He fished around for a few seconds and came up with a facecloth. "The last person I took a bath with wasn't potty-trained."

Char laughed. "Same here."

But her laughter died as he took the soaped-up facecloth and washed her throat and sides, coming ever closer to her breasts. His slow, steady movements augmented her already heightened sense of awareness. She strained forward, but he withdrew the facecloth, dropping it into the water again. Then, with his hand, he rinsed the soap off her skin, just skimming her breasts.

She couldn't stand it any longer. "Adam, we'll drown."

"But what a way to go."

He brushed a finger across each of her nipples, then cupped one breast, splaying his fingers as she moaned with a longing that seemed capable of making her explode. She slipped one arm under his and reached into the water for him, satisfied that he was throbbing with desire as much as she was. Her fingers moved with the same rhythm as his. He made small, guttural sounds in the back of his throat, then all at once pulled back.

"That's it, sweetheart. Out of the tub or damned if we don't drown."

She was already on her way. They grabbed towels, dried off in a hurry, and not very well. The chill of the bedroom air after the heat of the bath gave Char goose bumps and further excited her as she jumped into Adam's king-size bed, more luxurious than anything she had slept on in months. Adam joined her, and they snuggled under the blankets, warming each other with hands, feet, entwined legs, deep, hungry kisses.

"This feels so right," Char said, sliding underneath him, "and yet six months ago if someone had told me I'd be in Adam Stiles's bed tonight, I'd have prepared papers to have them committed."

All at once utterly serious, Adam said, "Maybe we both needed to be jolted out of the ordinariness of our lives to discover each other."

She nodded. "Maybe so."

They kissed slowly, erotically, hands and legs smoothing and probing and teasing. Then the tasting began, still slow, still erotic, until Char felt as if her entire being were filled with the scent and taste and sight of this man who was affecting her life in ways she couldn't have anticipated, wasn't even sure she wanted. Yet she wanted him as she had never wanted anyone else before . . . cared about him. To be with him she was prepared to throw away the old crystal ball she had for her life and fashion herself a new one.

She crawled onto his stomach and felt the tension— the wanting—in him. He didn't have to articulate what he was feeling. She could see his ambivalence, feel his wanting.

"It's all right," he said, as much to himself as to her, and lifted her hips, then eased her onto him.

Was it all right? What in blue blazes were she and Adam *doing*?

Then he moved inside her, and she sighed with acceptance and, at the same time, anticipation. "Yes—yes, it's all right."

She went with the moment, inhaling deeply as she set the pace for their lovemaking.

We're making love, she thought, *that's what we're doing*.

It was her last moderately coherent thought for what might have been minutes or hours. She didn't know; she didn't care. Time had no meaning. They threw off blankets and pillows, and any languor left over from their hot bath vanished with thrust after thrust, until they were breathing hard, moving faster and faster, crying out together.

She thought he might have yelled that he loved her, but she wasn't sure even what she herself had said. What did it matter? They were there, in bed together.

They remained joined for a long time, listening to their hearts beat and the fire crackle.

CHAR SLIPPED OUT OF BED early the next morning and got breakfast together. Adam being Adam, his kitchen was laid out in a logical manner: wherever Char looked for something first, there it was. She put on a pot of coffee, sliced a grapefruit and heated a couple of wild blueberry muffins in the microwave, waiting for the smell to get to Adam. It finally did, and he joined her in the kitchen.

"Quiet around here," he said.

"Mmm. Think we should call Julian and Holly and see if the kids lived through the night?"

"Probably should reverse that."

Char laughed and made the call. Everything was fine off in the woods. Julian and Holly weren't up yet, but Abby, David and Emily were all pitching in making pancakes and sausage. From scratch, Em said proudly. Char could just imagine. Adam warned them to clean up after themselves and promised he'd be by to pick them up soon.

"Have your kids ever made pancakes?" Char asked him when he'd hung up.

"No. Em?"

"Uh-uh."

"So long as they don't burn the place down, Julian and Holly won't care. But I guess we'd better get ourselves fed and dressed and rescue them before long. No homemade pancakes and sausages for us?"

"Reheated frozen muffins."

"Could be worse."

They ate on stools at the counter in the kitchen, Char practically inhaling her first cup of coffee. She poured another. "Adam, are you in a position to tell me what you and Harlan Rockwood talked about yesterday? I don't want to violate a confidence or put you in the middle, but..." She sighed, slipping back onto her stool with her fresh cup of coffee. "I would like to know where I can find the snake."

Adam's expression was unreadable, distant. "My guess is he's headed back to Tennessee."

"Why?"

"Because I told him that was where you were. I didn't know at the time you were on his tail."

"Oh." So she'd missed him: a thousand-mile trip for nothing. Well, she thought, not exactly nothing. "I see."

"Does that change your plans?"

"I didn't really have a plan. I just headed north when I found out he was in Millbrook and figured I'd play it by ear once I got here. So you think he was here because of me?"

"That was the impression I got," Adam said carefully. "He had no idea you were still living in Tennessee."

Char could feel her face coloring. "Thought he'd run me out of the state, did he?"

Adam cleared his throat. "I would say it's more complicated than that."

"Don't count on it," Char snapped, then immediately regretted her bad temper. "Sorry. I know you're trying not to take sides until all the facts are in, but I want an end to this thing with him so I can get on with my life. Right now . . . hell, I can barely think straight."

Easing himself off the stool, Adam refilled his mug, but didn't sit back down. He leaned against the counter, wearing nothing but a pair of jeans. Char even thought his toes were sexy.

"You do what you have to do," he said.

"You're not going to give me advice?"

"No."

"Even if I ask?"

He smiled. "You won't."

"But if I did."

"I told you, I'm not going to meddle."

For some reason that irritated Char. But she knew she would have been just as irritated if he had offered her unsolicited advice. "But don't you *want* me to do one thing instead of another?"

"No," he said, with surprising equanimity. "You do what you have to do. If you need to straighten out your business with Harlan before you can 'get on with your life,' then okay. If you don't, that's okay, too. I'm not going to make your decisions for you."

"I'm not asking you to," she countered. "It's just if you don't give a damn what I do—"

"I didn't say that."

"All right, all right. You're right. If you told me what to do and it turned out wrong, then I'd blame you. Even if it turned out right, I'd probably still blame you, wondering if I could have finished this thing on my own." She arched him a look. "But you do care?"

"Oh, yeah," he said. "I care."

He demonstrated just how much before they showered, dressed and went to fetch three children . . . in separate cars. Char had decided to head back to Tennessee.

"It's just something I have to do," she told Adam before they headed out to Julian and Holly's.

"I understand."

"You can tell me how you feel about it."

"How I feel isn't important."

She sighed. "It is to me."

With one finger he tilted up her chin and locked his eyes with hers. "I'll miss you" was all he said, but for Adam Stiles that was plenty.

On her way out of town Char stopped at the mill when she spotted Beth's bomb of a car in the parking lot. She almost drove straight on past, but Beth had to know her best friend was in Millbrook—and was no doubt wondering why she had chosen to stay with a Stiles male instead of the only Stiles female.

Beth, of course, knew everything that had happened in Millbrook within the past twenty-four hours: about Harlan's chat with her older brother, about Char's arrival, about Abby, David and Emily going off to stay with Holly and Julian while Char and Adam spent the night at his place, alone. Not a gossip herself, Beth was the sort of person in whom people confided. She had a way of finding out what she needed to know.

Char sent Emily off to play marbles in a far corner of the mill offices while Beth stood with her arms crossed, awaiting a well-deserved explanation.

"From the top," she told Char.

Taking a breath, Char complied. When she finished, Beth volunteered to join Char on her trip to Tennessee and help her skewer Harlan Rockwood.

Char politely declined her help. "The bottom line, Beth, is that I was swindled by your ex-husband and I'm in love with your brother, and I'm damned if I know what I'm going to do about either. But right now they're my problems, not yours." She smiled, and squeezed her friend's hand. "It's nice to know you're there if I need you. I—honestly, Beth, after Aunt Mil died I thought there was nothing left for me in Millbrook. Maybe I was wrong."

"That'd be a first," Beth muttered, then grinned, hugging Char and wishing her well.

Emily wasn't nearly as charitable: she felt cheated at having to leave Millbrook so soon and let her mother know so in no uncertain terms.

"Why can't we stay until tomorrow?" the seven-year-old demanded.

"Because we can't," Char said as she got her unwilling daughter back into the car. "Things didn't work out. The man I was supposed to see went back to Tennessee, and I've got to see him there."

"Will we be back?"

Char paused a moment, listening to the river rushing over the rocks and the wind in the brightly colored trees. "Yeah," she said, "we'll be back."

But a second-grader and only child of two attorneys wasn't one to be satisfied with such a vague answer. "When?"

"I don't know."

"Soon?"

Char felt the cool autumn breeze in her hair as she shut Em's door. "I hope so."

11

THE NEXT WEEK was one of the hardest in Adam's life. No tragedies were involved, as there had been in Mel's death and his own disabling accident. Instead there were dreams involved—hope, love, the future, all so elusive and unpredictable. All stuff he had forced himself to stop thinking about in terms of his own life, many, many months ago.

It was just a long week. Hellishly long.

He called Char every day, but she was close-mouthed about her affairs, although she did say that Harlan Rockwood remained in one piece. Adam judiciously kept quiet about his conversation with Harlan that day at the mill: he wondered if his former brother-in-law would remain in one piece if Char found out he had—and perhaps still did—suspected her of swindling him.

He ached to be in Tennessee with her. The distance he had tried to keep between himself and that fact slowly melted away during the week, and finally he admitted as much to Char.

"Just what I need," she muttered, "some Yankee mountain man swooping down here on his white horse."

But she had sounded pleased. And she had told him she would slay dragons for him, too.

He could have ignored her desire to straighten out her life on her own. He could hear the loneliness in her voice; he knew, in her way, she loved him. Yet he also knew Charity Bradford was proud and stubborn and had risked more than most would dare and lost more than most could stand. She had a right to straighten out her life on her own.

"Has word hit the streets that we spent the night together?" she asked.

"It was on the front page of the paper."

He worked and took Abby and David apple picking and talked to them about how Mel would always be their mother, no matter what Adam did with the rest of his life. They seemed already to know that.

He looked into frequent-flyer benefits in case Char decided to stay in Tennessee and they would have to have a long-distance relationship.

He checked out buying a travel van.

He considered ways he could restructure his responsibilities at the mill to include more time in Tennessee, working around Abby and David's schedules.

He studied horses.

And he daydreamed. That was a new experience for him. He would sit at his desk and imagine Char coming through the door, imagine her dark doe's eyes flashing, imagine how he would ask her to marry him.

Craziness. But his daydreaming helped pass the time.

By Friday afternoon he had resigned himself to a long weekend ahead, and an even longer week. He dug into his work.

Beth, who had been uncharacteristically quiet all week, slid into the leather chair by his desk. "Have you heard? Somebody's rented Char's old office."

"I guess it was bound to happen. It's a good location."

"I heard it was a lawyer."

Adam felt his jaw stiffening. "The town could use another lawyer."

"Char's shoes won't be easy to fill."

"No," he said in agreement, surprised at how awful he had felt. However unrealistic, he had hoped that in straightening out her life, Char would decide to return to Millbrook and her law practice—on her own, without any pressure from him. Now even if she did decide to come home, she would have competition. It might not be so easy to pick up the pieces of her old life.

"You want me to find out more?" Beth asked.

Adam shook his head. "There's no need."

So much for out-of-hand dreams, he thought. For now he'd better stick to reality.

THE BRIGHTEST REDS AND ORANGES had fallen from the trees, but southern Vermont was still crowded with leaf-peepers. With Emily singing beside her, Char picked her way through the clogged traffic in downtown Millbrook. *This* time her car wouldn't be spotted: her old hatchback couldn't make another thousand-mile trip within a week. She'd traded it in for a newer model. Another time of year the Tennessee license plate might have been a dead giveaway, but not during leaf-peeping season.

"Are we going to stay with Uncle Adam?" Emily asked.

"I don't know. Maybe."

"Abby and David said they're making cider this weekend."

Char could almost smell its sweetness. "Maybe they'll let you help."

Satisfied, Emily resumed singing. To entertain herself on the long trip north, she had resorted to singing every song she had ever learned, from nursery school on up to second grade. She seemed to have worked her way into kindergarten, but Char couldn't be sure if Em had finished one cycle and had started all over again. Good mother that she was, she had tuned out her daughter's singing sometime around Wytheville, Virginia.

There wasn't a parking space to be had on Main Street. Millbrook natives could park at Hank's Garage without fear of being towed, but Hank couldn't reasonably be trusted to let an unfamiliar car with Tennessee plates off. Char turned off Main, circled the block and came up and tried again. After two attempts she finally landed a space practically in front of her old office.

It was Emily who first spotted the restoration of Charity W. Bradford, Attorney-at-Law to the signpost. If her car wouldn't start gossip, her name back in place certainly would. By her instruction, however, it had been put there no earlier than midafternoon.

"*Mom!*"

Char grinned at her daughter. "I didn't know you could read."

Emily took a moment to scowl at her mother before racing into the building. There, as Char had instructed her mover, a former client's son, her office furniture had been pulled out of storage and set up, if somewhat haphazardly. She unlocked the place and peered in, feeling more satisfaction than terror, although there was a little of that, too.

"My shingle's all dusted off and ready to be nailed up again," she said, leaning against the doorframe while Emily explored. "Your mom the lawyer."

"Can I have my old shelf back?"

Em had always had one shelf in her mother's office reserved for her things, provided they weren't living. "Of course."

For days Em had been flying high because they were moving back to Millbrook, but Char had withheld details on exactly how they were going to survive. She'd had to get used to the idea of returning to her law practice herself. Now it felt fine, sort of like climbing back into a favorite raggedy sweatshirt and a pair of jeans after an arduous diet.

"Where are we going to live?" Em, ever practical, asked.

Char sighed. "I've got a line on a cottage within walking distance of town for rent, but for now . . ." She thought of Adam, and her stomach muscles tightened. "I'm working on it."

ADAM HAD LEFT the mill early to pick up ten bushels of apples for Saturday's cider-making extravaganza. It was his turn to host this year. Julian would bring the press, Beth the containers, Holly the makings for cider doughnuts and hot mulled cider. In addition to his mountain of utility-grade apples, Adam would provide lunch and supper. He had plates of cold cuts and raw vegetables in the refrigerator, two big pans of lasagna he'd made and stuck in the freezer before Nashville and Charity Bradford, salad, garlic bread and baked apples.

With his hook in place he opened the tailgate on his truck and grabbed one of the baskets of apples, setting it on the edge of the driveway. He hardly paused before snatching the next basket.

He worked furiously, sweating and cursing. There wasn't any hurry: no foreman on a timetable, no forecasts of rain, nowhere else to go. But he had always relied on hard work to keep distractions at bay.

Damn it, he thought, *I hate gossip.*

One of the sawyers at the mill had heard around three o'clock that Char's name had been replaced on a signpost in front of the Stiles building in town.

Someone's idea of a joke, Adam assumed. The town was having a hell of a time passing along the news that crusty old one-handed Adam Stiles and sharp, cranky Charity Bradford had a thing going.

He wasn't in the mood to laugh.

A car turned into his driveway, but he ignored it, leaning into the truck to grab another basket of apples. Probably just some leaf-peeper using his driveway to turn around. But he heard the car make the hill up to the house, and when he turned around, it was practically at his heels.

A dark blue compact. Strangers, he thought. He supposed he'd have to be sociable.

Then Char poked her dark head out of the driver's window and grinned at him. "You give up the mill and go into the apple business?"

He couldn't speak. Emily was already bounding out of the car, and when she asked where Abby and David were, he managed to grunt something about their being in their tree house. He could have put them to work unloading the truck, of course, but he had wanted the job all to himself.

Char climbed out of the car, dressed in jeans and a fisherman's sweater and as gorgeous and elusive as he had ever seen her.

Partially recovered, Adam took out a bushel of apples, set it on the ground, then leaned back against his truck. Char was licking her lips and obviously waiting for him to say something. Too bad, he thought. It's your move, sweetheart.

"Had my phone disconnected," she said, brushing her hands on the sides of her thighs. "Otherwise I'd have called and let you know I was coming."

"Could have called collect."

"Well, I didn't."

She hopped onto the tailgate and snatched up a stray apple, biting into it with that mix of energy and calm—that one-track-mind intensity—that had been uniquely hers since childhood.

Adam didn't move. "You want to tell me what you're up to?"

She motioned with her apple. "I bought a new car."

"So I see. Char, if you're going to send me on some kind of wild-goose chase—"

"Me?"

She seemed so surprised, so appalled at the idea, that anyone who hadn't been sent to Belle Meade, Cheekwood and the Rockwood estate would have immediately backed off.

"We have a history," Adam said dryly.

"That sounds ominous." Her tone suggested it didn't sound ominous at all. She took another bite of apple, swinging her legs. "I looked for you at the mill."

"Came home early."

"Yeah, Beth told me about the cider bash tomorrow. She also told me you busted out of there like a man on fire. Something up?"

He narrowed his eyes at her, refusing to rise to her so-tempting bait. "You tell me."

She shrugged. "Thought you might have heard a rumor."

"I don't listen to gossip."

"Sometimes you have no choice. You hear I was in town?"

"No."

"Then you must have heard my shingle was back up on the States building. True?"

He sighed. "True?"

"When did you hear?"

"Char—"

"No, I'm curious. My name went up at two o'clock this afternoon. I'm just wondering how long it takes for word to travel in this town."

"I heard at three."

"An hour. Amazing."

She took another bite of apple, then laid back and heaved the core off into the woods.

"Start talking, Char," Adam said, "or next I'll toss you into the woods."

"It's chilly. Want to finish unloading the truck and go inside where it's warm?"

"And give you time to rewrite whatever tale you're going to tell me? No way. We'll talk right here."

She made a face. "The brain functions best at fifty-eight degrees, anyway."

The woman, Adam thought, had the look of victory about her—as if the weight of the world had finally been lifted from her shoulders. Clearly something was up. But he refused to prompt her. This, he thought, was her show.

"Harlan Rockwood and I came to an agreement," she said. Before she continued, she angled her eyes at Adam. "Did you know he suspected *me* of swindling *him?*"

"I'll take the Fifth."

"I bet you will. Anyway, finding that out made me take a look at this thing from a new angle. If I didn't swindle Harlan and Harlan didn't swindle me, what *did* happen? I launched a little investigation of my own. Harlan got wind of it, and we decided to put our heads together, which you will not tell Beth. We discovered that one of his trainers—a guy who'd been with him maybe three years—switched our horse with a ringer and sold our star to an outfit in Europe and passed the dud off. The switch might have been discovered sooner if Harlan had continued to race the dud, but he got disgusted and put him out to pasture."

"And you were each looking to the other for blame while the trainer went about his business."

"That's pretty much the long and short of it."

"So what about your money?"

She got a distant look in her beautiful brown eyes. "Oh, Harlan and I worked that out."

"Are you going to try again at raising Thoroughbreds?"

"Nope."

It seemed so easy, as if she were saying, "No, she didn't want green beans for supper."

"I have no regrets," she went on. "But my dream of raising Thoroughbreds has to do with the kid I used to be, not the woman I've become. When Aunt Mil died I felt so empty. I'm not sure I would have admitted this a year ago, but my leaving Millbrook had everything to do with her death—and not just because she left me the means to go. I thought I was just seizing the moment to make a dream come true. To some degree, I was, but it was more complicated than that. I wasn't just running to something, but away from something."

"Away from Millbrook," Adam said.

"Away from what Millbrook had become for me without Aunt Mil." Char brought her feet up onto the tailgate and tucked her knees under her chin. "There's a difference. I felt so damn alone, Adam. And I didn't think I could tell anyone, just as I couldn't tell anyone about my disastrous deal with Harlan. I was wrong. I still have friends—a life—here in Millbrook."

"Is it the life you want?"

She looked at him with an expression that just dared him to argue. "Yes."

He argued, anyway. "Char, you've been itching to get out of Millbrook since you were a kid."

"And I got out. You'll also recall I came back after my divorce."

"You had to."

"I did not have to. I could easily have stayed in New York, but I chose to come back here."

"You *said*—"

She waved a hand in dismissal. "I was an idiot."

Adam crossed his arms on his chest. "You're not coming back on my account?"

"Not *just* on your account. Adam, when I left last week a part of me wanted you to jump to my side and solve all my problems for me—to make demands. Then I'd be off the hook. But I'm glad you kept your distance and let me come to terms with what *I* wanted on my own. Yeah, it helps that I don't have to come home with my tail tucked all the way between my legs. Finding out a knowledgeable horse breeder like Harlan Rockwood was swindled just the same as me was a boost to my ego, never mind to my pocketbook."

She dropped her legs down and let them swing, her hands gripping the end of the tailgate. "And it helps that you're here. I'm not going to pretend it doesn't. But I didn't come back to Millbrook just for you. I came back for me, too."

Adam felt the tension in his arms and legs, in his entire body. "You're sure?"

"It's practically all I've thought about since I left here last Saturday, and believe me, I had to think or go crazy listening to Em sing 'That Chubby Little Snowman' between Hagerstown and Roanoke." She smiled. "So, yes, I'm sure."

"We'd have worked something out no matter what you decided," Adam said, encircling her waist with his arms.

She nodded. "I know we would have."

"I'd have bought a sawmill in Tennessee if it'd come to that."

"It never would have. I wouldn't want the burden of forcing you to do something against your nature—to become someone else—anymore than you do."

He smiled, easing her into his arms and down off the truck. "Your nose is red. We'd better go inside and warm up."

"There is one more thing. I've heard from an ex-client who's thinking about suing Mill Brook Post & Beam."

"Who?"

"I can't give you any details—client confidentiality and all that." She slid her hands up his back and locked those dark eyes on him. "I'd like to tell him I can't handle the case due to conflict of interest. What do you think?"

"I'm not a lawyer."

She gave him a long suffering sigh. "Adam Stiles, you can be such a thickheaded Yankee. If I'm sleeping with the president of Mill Brook Post & Beam, don't you think I have a conflict of interest?"

He drew her tightly against him and lowered his mouth to hers. "I'd say you have a hell of a conflict of interest."

THE FOLLOWING SPRING Char chose the day of the running of the Kentucky Derby to announce the wedding date for her marriage to Adam Stiles. They hosted a party at his house and invited most of the town. There were kids and adults everywhere. The actual wedding ceremony, she and Adam had decided by mutual agreement, would be quiet and private, with just family in attendance. On her own initiative Abby had asked the Eberharts if they could hold the ceremony among Aunt Mil's peonies and irises. The Eberharts were delighted to comply.

Aunt Mil, Char thought, would have approved.

Most of the party-goers went home to watch the race in peace. Everyone else—except for the kids, who couldn't get excited about a bunch of horses they didn't know running around a circle—gathered around the television set in Adam's family room.

Adam slipped an arm around his fiancée. "Feel a twinge of regret you're not there?"

"Just a twinge," Char admitted. It was a bald-faced lie: only the scheme she'd cooked up in the past few weeks had made not being in Lexington today the least bit palatable. Now if everything fell into place... Well, she couldn't think about consequences right now. The truth was, if Beth didn't strangle her, Adam would.

"You're awfully tense," her future husband observed.

"I always get tense for horse races."

"Yeah, but...Char, are you up to something again?"

"Shh! There's the gun."

Char jumped up and down and yelled so loud that everyone else missed the name of the winning horse. So, choking back her glee, she calmed herself and told them. "Stubborn Yankee."

Beth went pale. "What did you say?"

Char repeated it for her, just as the television reporter stuck a microphone toward the ecstatic owner.

Harlan Rockwood smiled his charmer's smile for all of North America to see.

Beth was on her feet. "*That snake!*"

"Now, Beth," Char said, "don't judge him too fast. Remember our deal last fall?"

Beth was biting her nails. "Yeah, yeah," she said impatiently. "I let you invest my twenty grand in another horse scheme and agreed not to tell the Stiles men about it. That's got nothing to do with having to watch my ex-husband on television. Lord, doesn't he look so smug?"

Adam cleared his throat, but Char ignored him. "Beth, there's something I neglected to tell you. I would have, of course, but you're so unreasonable when it comes to Harlan and, anyway, God forbid I should learn from one mistake."

"Uh-oh," Adam said, just as his sister flew around at her best friend.

"Char, don't tell me. *Please* don't tell me."

But Char was too pleased with herself not to tell her. "I used what money I needed to get back on my feet and invested the rest of what I had in another horse Harlan had high hopes for. That horse that just won the Kentucky Derby? Beth, *we* own part of that horse. Our share amounts to maybe a hoof, but it's ours."

"Well, Stubborn Yankee," Adam said to his sister, laughing, "what do you think of that?"

This time it was Char who looked confused. "Stubborn Yankee is the name of the horse that just won."

"It was also," Beth said in disgust, "my ex-husband's nickname for me when we first met in college."

"You're kidding?"

From Beth's look, Char could see she wasn't kidding.

"Oh, dear," Char said.

Adam, however, wasn't taking his sister's mortification seriously at all. "Why don't you go down to Tennessee and pick up your winnings in person, Beth? You're due time off at the mill."

She scowled at her older brother. "That snake in the grass would slither off the second he saw me coming."

"I don't know," Adam said, amused, "seems to me you and Mr. Rockwood have unfinished business, even after all this time."

"I'll say we have unfinished business," Beth said ominously.

"And Char can't go."

"What do you mean, I can't go?" Char jumped in. "I don't have anything pressing on my calendar, and I'll speak for myself, thank you."

"Don't go getting all hot under the collar. I just thought you might want to be around to help me put up our barn."

Char went still, thoroughly confused now. "*Our* barn? Adam Stiles, what are you talking about?"

"An old-fashioned post-and-beam barn. I've ordered a kit for us. It's sort of an engagement present."

"A barn," Char said unenthusiastically, but her heart was filled with warmth for this sturdy, practical man she adored. "How typically Yankee, Adam. Honestly. Most men give their fiancées diamonds. Me, I get a barn."

"I didn't say the barn was a present for you."

"It's for you?"

"And the kids. What goes in the barn's for you."

"I'm not even going to guess," she said.

He slid his arms around her and held her close. "A friend of mine raises Morgans up near Montpelier. We've worked out a deal, and he has a colt for you to look at, if you're interested."

"Interested?" Char threw her arms around his neck. "Oh, Adam, I love you."

"I've got a team coming in the morning to start clearing some land out back," he said. "Speechless for a change, darling? If you can keep a secret from me, I can keep one from you."

"Adam . . ." But she couldn't go on. She *was* speechless.

"You can still have your dreams, love," he said softly.

"You're my best dream."

"I hope so. I'd hate to be beaten out by a horse, even a Derby winner."

"I would have told you."

"And spoil all your fun? Not a chance. Char, my love, I do know you."

"Then I gather you're not going to strangle me?"

He laughed. "That's not exactly what I had in mind."

And he kissed her on the mouth, right there in front of everyone.

From the author of
DADDY, DARLING

DOCTOR, DARLING
by
Glenda Sanders

The eagerly awaited sequel to DADDY,
DARLING is here! In DOCTOR, DARLING,
the imposing Dr. Sergei Karol meets his match.
He's head over heels in love with Polly
Mechler, the adorable TV celebrity whose
plumbing-supply commercials have made her
a household name. But Sergei wants Polly to
be adorable just for him . . . and Polly isn't one
to follow doctor's orders!

Watch for DOCTOR, DARLING.
Coming in January 1991

TDDR

History is now twice as exciting, twice as romantic!

Harlequin is proud to announce that, by popular demand, Harlequin Historicals will be increasing from two to four titles per month, starting in February 1991.

Even if you've never read a historical romance before, you will love the great stories you've come to expect from favorite authors like Patricia Potter, Lucy Elliot, Ruth Langan and Heather Graham Pozzessere.

Enter the world of Harlequin Historicals and share the adventures of cowboys and captains, pirates and princes.

*Available wherever
Harlequin books are sold.*

HARLEQUIN
American Romance®

RELIVE THE MEMORIES....

From New York's immigrant experience to San Francisco's Great Quake of '06. From the western front of World War I to the Roaring Twenties. From the indomitable spirit of the thirties to the home front of the Fabulous Forties to the baby-boom fifties . . . A CENTURY OF AMERICAN ROMANCE takes you on a nostalgic journey.

From the turn of the century to the dawn of the year 2000, you'll revel in the romance of a time gone by and sneak a peek at romance in an exciting future.

Watch for all the CENTURY OF AMERICAN ROMANCE titles coming to you one per month over the next four months in Harlequin American Romance.

Don't miss a day of A CENTURY OF AMERICAN ROMANCE.

A CENTURY OF
AMERICAN ROMANCE
1960s

The women . . . the men . . . the passions . . . the memories . . .

Harlequin Intrigue®

REBECCA YORK

Labeled a "true master of intrigue" by *Rave Reviews*, best-selling author Rebecca York makes her Harlequin Intrigue debut with an exciting suspenseful new series.

43
Light St.

It looks like a charming old building near the renovated Baltimore waterfront, but inside 43 Light Street lurks danger . . . and romance.

Let Rebecca York introduce you to:

> *Abby Franklin*—a psychologist who risks everything to save a tough adventurer determined to find the truth about his sister's death. . . .
>
> *Jo O'Malley*—a private detective who finds herself matching wits with a serial killer who makes her his next target. . . .
>
> *Laura Roswell*—a lawyer whose inherited share in a development deal lands her in the middle of a murder. And she's the chief suspect. . . .

These are just a few of the occupants of 43 Light Street you'll meet in Harlequin Intrigue's new ongoing series. Don't miss any of the 43 LIGHT STREET books, beginning with #143 LIFE LINE.

And watch for future LIGHT STREET titles, including #155 SHATTERED VOWS (February 1991) and #167 WHISPERS IN THE NIGHT (August 1991).

HI-143-1

HARLEQUIN Temptation

COMING NEXT MONTH

#329 DOCTOR, DARLING Glenda Sanders
(Spinoff from #257 *Daddy, Darling*)

Dr. Sergei Karol was no mere mortal. He was a
microsurgeon, the man who'd saved Polly Mechler's brother
from a disability injury. And Polly... well, Polly was cute,
and she sold plumbing supplies on TV. The great Dr. Karol
had yet to discover that Polly wasn't adorable just for him.
She was a celebrity—and her fame was about to spread
nationwide....

#330 CHANCE IT Joanna Gilpin

Diane Roberts was selling off her real-estate empire and
setting out for adventure. And adventure beckoned in the
form of dynamic Ira Nicholson. On his yacht they set sail on
a course of sensual exploration—with the strict
understanding that this was a temporary affair. Too late, the
cool-headed businesswoman realized she had badly
miscalculated her own heart.

#331 EASY LOVIN' Candace Schuler

Prim and proper Kate Hightower had never fancied herself
as a runaway bride. Yet here she was, in New Orleans,
thousands of miles away from her fiancé, in very *unsuitable*
company. Jesse de Vallerin oozed with Southern charm and
seemed determined to teach Kate how to "loosen up." Were
her jitters just the prenuptial kind... or the result of Jesse's
easy lovin'?

#332 DIFFERENT WORLDS
Elaine K. Stirling (Book I-Lovers Apart)

Dawn Avery's life was her work in the rain forests of Central
America. Michael Garrett was committed to a career in
Western Canada. Their worlds collided in a brief, passionate
affair in Costa Rica that left them breathless, aching for
more. Fate had brought them together. But could their love
go the distance...?